TOM SWIFT™

young inventor

#3 THE SPACE HOTEL

By Victor Appleton

Aladdin Paperbacks
New York London Toronto Sydney

visit us at www.abdopublishing.com

Reinforced library bound edition published in 2008 by Spotlight, a division of ABDO Publishing Group, 8000 West 78th Street, Edina, Minnesota 55439. Published by agreement with Aladdin Paperbacks, an imprint of Simon & Schuster Children's Publishing Division.

🫖 ALADDIN PAPERBACKS
An imprint of Simon & Schuster Children's Publishing Division
1230 Avenue of the Americas, New York, NY 10020

Designed by Lisa Vega

Library of Congress Cataloging-in-Publication Data

This title was previously cataloged with the following information:

Appleton, Victor.
   Space Hotel / Victor Appleton.
     p. cm. -- (Tom Swift, young inventor ; #3)
     I. Title. II. Series: Tom Swift, young inventor ; #3.

[Fic]--dc22   2006931755

ISBN 978-1-59961-353-6 (reinforced library bound edition)

All Spotlight books are reinforced library binding
and manufactured in the United States of America.

Contents

Ups and Downs

"Check it out, Sandy," I said, looking at my younger sister upside down. Like a spider, I used my fingers and feet to slowly "walk" across the padded surface of the plane's ceiling and then back again. "I've always wanted to be a 'fly on the wall'!"

Sandy looked up at me. She was hovering in a cross-legged sitting position a good six inches off the plane's floor. "Ho, ho, ho, it's Tom Swift Jr., the king of comedy," she replied into her Swift Speak, the miniature microphone-and-earpiece combo that allowed us to communicate in normal voices over the roar of the plane's engines. "Just don't fall on me when the plane finishes its arc!"

We were passengers aboard the *SwiftStar*, the latest invention of my dad's business, Swift Enterprises.

It was a special jet astronauts used to get a feel for what it would be like to be in outer space, where there was very little gravity. Microgravity, it was called. Scientists used the plane too; some of their experiments work best in a weightless environment.

My dad showed Sandy and me the plans for the plane months ago, and it didn't take long for me to become as excited about it as he was. "The plane's the size of a small air tanker," he explained, pointing to diagrams on the paper. "It'll make a steep, graceful climb to a high altitude, then descend in that same arc."

Sandy nodded. "Coming down, the people inside will become weightless!"

"You got it, Sandy," Dad said, squeezing her shoulder. "But only for about a minute."

"A minute?!" I repeated, unable to believe my ears. "That's more than twice the time you can float in a 'Vomit Comet'!"

My dad was too caught up in the excitement of the project to realize I had called the plane that the air force and NASA used for the same purpose by the nickname they used. "And the 'Vom . . .'" He paused, catching himself. He cleared his throat and scratched his graying temple. "The plane the government uses can only make thirty to forty parabolas," he said, dipping his hand up and down to mimic the plane's flight path. "The *SwiftStar* has increased fuel capacity, so it can stay in the air for six hours!"

"Twice the ups and downs, twice the training!" I said, shaking my head.

"And twice the science," Sandy added.

"Sweet!" I exclaimed.

"Sweet, indeed," Dad said, nodding firmly.

Suddenly, my arms and legs felt as heavy as oak tree logs—gravity was coming back. Captain Lisa Ryder's voice crackled over the plane's intercom. She was Swift Enterprises' chief test pilot. "How's my honorary crew?" she shouted above the engines' roar, and I could tell from the way she said it that she was smiling. "Anybody need an airsickness bag?"

"No problems back here, Lisa, we're floating like feathers," I answered lightly . . . then bumped my head against the fuselage. Good thing the main cabin of the plane was heavily padded. For takeoffs and landings, we'd be strapped in to the traditional airplane seats that were in the rear cabin. And they were safely bolted down.

A member of the *SwiftStar's real* crew smiled at

Sandy and me. He was there in case one of us got hurt, or sick. "Feet down, coming out," he yelled.

I stretched out my legs and grabbed on to a padded handle on the side of the fuselage. My feet lightly touched the floor, then slowly gained more and more weight. Even though I'd only been weightless for less than a minute, it felt like a sumo wrestler was pressing down on the top of my shoulders. All of a sudden I found myself missing that free-floating sensation and I couldn't wait for that feeling again. Once you'd had the chance to fly, it was hard to give it up, even for a little while.

Sandy, too, drifted down to the floor of the plane, her legs still crossed in a sitting position. She grasped handles set into the floor on either side of her. "What's the deal?" I asked her. "You just sat when we went zero-G! Why weren't you bouncing around and having fun?"

"I was studying," she answered patiently, "trying to figure out the most efficient ways to move." That's my little sister, more into the science than the coolness. A real firecracker.

The plane started to climb again into another arc, and I felt my full weight return—and then increase. We were climbing at an angle of forty-five degrees, so steep, I felt almost twice as heavy as usual, to the point where it was even hard to hold myself up.

"Ready for float," the crewman shouted after half a minute, and the *SwiftStar* leveled out, then dipped toward the ground again. All sense of weight disappeared, and my toes lifted off the floor once more into the total freedom of weightlessness. I let go of the handle and let myself drift, as though in a lake on a lazy summer afternoon.

I watched as Sandy rose off the floor in her sitting position, then unfolded her legs and reached up for one of the handles lining the walls. She tested her grip for a second, then pulled herself past the handle, her momentum propelling her forward until she reached the next handle, and the one after that, and the one after that. She "swung" the length of the cabin and back faster than I could have walked! She took a handle across the cabin from me when she got back. "That seemed pretty efficient, didn't it?" she asked.

I had to try it myself. If Sandy could do it . . . I stretched out parallel to the floor, still holding the handle. I took a deep breath, then pulled myself forward and pushed off, moving far faster than Sandy had been going. Unfortunately, I was going *too* fast, and

5

missed the next handle, swiping at it in vain. I flailed my arms like a drowning man, and tumbled end over end the length of the cabin before thumping into the padding at its end. I bounced off and hung in the air upside down, dazed. "Sure didn't feel efficient," I muttered sheepishly.

"You've gotta take your time," Sandy called out to me, pointing to her belly button. "Make sure your line of motion runs through your center of gravity at all times, and just go handle to handle and don't worry about speed. . . . That'll take care of itself!"

I decided to try it her way, took another deep breath, and reached for the closest handle. Wouldn't you know, I made it back to my starting point without breaking any bones or looking too stupid. "Pretty cool," I admitted. "That'll make getting around a lot easier on our vacation!"

The crewmember raised an eyebrow. "You're going on holiday in the *SwiftStar*?" he asked loudly.

"Even better," I shouted back excitedly. I could feel the weight returning to my arms and legs—and I could feel myself wanting to be back in microgravity as soon as possible. "We're going on vacation two hundred and thirty-six thousand miles from Earth!"

The First Wild Ride

Sandy and I stepped out of the Rio de Janeiro airport and were met with a blast of damp, hot air. Instantly, my clothes started to stick to my skin, and a thin sweat broke out across my forehead, down my neck, and into the small of my back. I felt like I was breathing soup rather than oxygen. Didn't Brazil know this was November? Of course, this close to the equator, the temperature hardly moved a degree in either direction.

Taxis, cars, and limousines crawled past us. Polluted haze covered the mountains in the distance. Rio has the reputation of being one of the most fun, wild, and crazy cities on the planet, with its beaches and crowded nightclubs, but I sure couldn't tell that by the airport on a stifling hot afternoon, that's for sure.

The heat was starting to make my eyelids droop. Sandy was half awake, having slept all the way from home. She has that gift, the ability to fall asleep anywhere, at any time, regardless of the situation. I'm not much of a sleeper on planes to begin with, and besides, I was too hyped up about our upcoming "vacation" to even think about sleeping. But now, the miles were catching up with me, and that, combined with the heat, was about to make me drop into a nap whether I wanted one or not. And I really didn't want that, not with all I was about to experience!

Sandy let out a huge yawn. "Stop it," I begged her. "You know yawning's contagious!" And with that, I yawned twice as hugely as my sister, unable to help myself.

"It's your own fault," Sandy chided me. "If you'd just learn how to relax, you'd have slept on the plane like me, and you'd be ready to go now."

I was just grumpy enough that we might have gotten into a full-blown sibling argument, but a black limousine made a daring cut through two lanes of traffic and screeched to a halt right in front of us. The cars all around it honked in disbelief. The noise woke me up . . . a little.

"Whoa," Sandy and I said at the same time.

The driver's side door opened, and a short, fat Brazilian man hopped out, wearing a driver's cap, a blue blazer . . . and a Hawaiian shirt beneath. *I'll be professional*, his outfit seemed to say, *but only to a point.*

He looked at us and smiled, revealing a gold front tooth. He held up a sign that read, TOM AND SANDY SWIFT. He pointed at us, pointed to his sign, and nodded. "This is you? You are this?" he asked, with a heavy Portuguese accent.

"More or less," I replied. He hadn't needed to even ask the question since Sandy and I were wearing Swift Enterprises T-shirts.

He bounded up onto the curb and shook both our hands with vigorous energy. "I am late and I apologize," he said. "My name is Joao, and I am your driver. I will be taking you to the Launch Lobby."

"*¿Como é você*, Joao?" Sandy asked. She'd been practicing her Portuguese for a week before we left, and was obviously happy for the chance to show off.

Joao was clearly impressed, smiling even more broadly and bowing. "I am well, Miss Swift! Thank you for asking!"

"*Seu nome é* Sandy," I told him, formally introducing

9

my sister. I'd been practicing my Portuguese too. *"Meu nome é* Tom."

Now he bowed to me as well, equally impressed. "It is a pleasure to meet you both, Tom and Sandy Swift," he said. When he said "Swift," it sounded like "Swiff." He turned and gestured to the car. "Now that we all know one another, may I suggest we go? We have a long drive ahead of us."

He took my duffel bag and Sandy's—neither of which was exactly light—and loaded them with ease into the car's trunk. We climbed into the back, and I sank down into the comfortable leather seat. *Good thing it's a long drive,* I thought. *Maybe I actually will get some sleep.*

Joao slid behind the driver's seat, put the car in gear, and put the gas pedal to the floor! The car lurched forward and sideways, right into moving traffic, sliding just barely into the open space between a truck and a motor scooter, setting off a flurry of honks!

Joao looked over his shoulder and grinned at us as he drove without paying any attention to the road, miraculously managing to avoid smacking into any cars, guardrails . . . or people. "I was sorry to hear your parents were not coming," he said. "I would have liked very much to meet Mister Doctor Tom Swift Sr.!"

"He and our mom were too busy," I said, instinctively ducking and dodging while sitting in my seat.

Joao nodded. "You are excited to see the Apogee Space Hotel, right?"

I grabbed on to the door handle, my knuckles turning white. Next to me, Sandy did the same. Maybe Joao couldn't see where he was going, but *we* could. Cars swerved away on either side of us, and we could see the angry, terrified faces of the drivers who were barely escaping with their lives. "Very excited," Sandy said. "I just hope we actually get to *see* it!"

I did too. Ever since Dad had told me about the first "space hotel," I couldn't wait to lay eyes on it!

The idea of tourism extending into space was a no-brainer. It's man's nature to explore, Dad liked to say, and as long as there are new things to see and do, people will want to see and do them. Ever since astronauts had first gone into orbit, "normal folks" had dreamed of the chance to see what outer space was like.

For a long time, many design firms had debated the best approach to building a space hotel, but recently, in the last few years, everyone had agreed on the basic idea. At its core, the hotel would have a solid metal cylinder, housing all the "operations" aspects of the facility: the Command Center, the kitchen, the laundry, the docking bays for transport shuttles, and so on. The core would also feature a series of air locks, into which would attach as many inflatable "modules" as the structure could accommodate. These would be the "guest rooms," and in them would be not only sleeping quarters, but dining rooms, libraries, gyms, and, of course, observation decks offering stupendous views of Earth below and the stars all around. While on the hotel, guests and crew would live in microgravity—essentially weightless!

It sounded too fantastic to be true, but it was. Lots of companies had raced to be the first to get a hotel into space, among them Swift Enterprises' chief rival, the sneaky Foger Utility Group, or FUG. But a company called Above and Beyond, with backing, technology, and materials from Swift Enterprises, which was a major investor in the project, had crossed the finish line first with the Apogee Space Hotel.

Apogee was about to open for business, and we were going to be among the very first guests! Soon, lots of people would fly shuttles to hotels that soared above the highest levels of the atmosphere, and we'd be able to tell them what to expect.

"Oh, Apogee is very impressive," Joao said casually, resting his wrist atop the steering wheel. It seemed like we were going even faster, now that we were out of the airport roads and into regular city traffic, which was even more congested. Half seriously, I wondered if it was possible that Joao was actually some sort of new android, outfitted with a guidance chip.

"You've *been* to Apogee?" I asked, my head whipping from side to side with every near collision. Suddenly it seemed like *everyone* was driving like Joao! Cars turned and twisted every which way, avoiding disaster by a hair's width, continuing to drive at recklessly high speeds. Honks came from every direction, but no one seemed to pay much attention to them. Steering with one hand and honking with the other seemed to be as much a part of everyday driving here as stepping on the gas or brake. Maybe you *had* to drive like this to live in Brazil!

Joao shook his head. "No, no," he replied. "I haven't been to Apogee . . . but I have seen pictures! I've worked for Above and Beyond for many years. Very, *very* impressive!"

We rode in silence for the next several miles, Sandy and I on high alert for possible crashes, Joao simply humming along to himself as though nothing were out of the ordinary. I suppose, to him, nothing was. When we cleared the city limits for the rural highway, my sister and I relaxed a little. There were far fewer cars here, and while there was the occasional rickety truck carrying produce or livestock, we felt much safer. "It is about three hours to the Launch Lobby," Joao said pleasantly. "Please relax. Maybe sleep?"

Yeah, not a chance. I settled back in the seat, accepting the intermittent swervings and honkings, but definitely not comfortable. I turned to look out the window at the Brazilian countryside rolling by. Between that, the hum of the engine, and the wave-like curving of the road, however, sleep came to get me, whether I wanted to go or not. I fell into a deep and heavy doze and dreamed of flying in outer space.

Surrounded

"Tom? Tom, wake up!"

The voice seemed to come to me through a thick, gray fog. I had a terrible pain in my neck and left shoulder—I had fallen asleep wedged against the limousine's door. My eyes opened with a little pop. It felt like my eyelids had been glued shut, almost.

Sandy was shaking me awake, and her eyes were wide and frightened. It takes a *lot* to scare my little sister—she doesn't freak out easily. "Tom, what do they want?"

As my murky brain tried to process the information it was receiving, I struggled to sit up straight, my neck and shoulder protesting. It was dark in the car, for some reason, like we had stopped halfway through a tunnel. I caught a quick look at myself in Joao's rearview mirror: thanks to the heat and my awkward position, all the hair on the left side of my head was sticking straight up. I looked like one half of my body had been plugged into a light socket.

Joao's eyes caught mine, and he shook his head slightly, as though apologizing. "This is very, very bad," he said.

Not sure what to expect, I turned my head to look out the window—and found myself looking into the eyes of a madman! Or maybe it only looked that way. He was pressed against the glass, his features flattened out, his eyes bulging and sweat pouring down his face. He was yelling something, but I couldn't hear through the window. Next to him was another face. And behind them, another. Quickly, I looked to the other side of the limo. More angry-looking people pressed against the car from that side. There were others on the hood, pushing against the windshield. That was why it seemed so dark in the car—it was completely surrounded, enveloped, and covered by human beings!

"Who are they?" Sandy wanted to know, a touch of hysteria in her voice.

It was Joao who answered. "They do not want to see Apogee open," he said. "They are from an organization that calls themselves 'The Road Back.'"

The Road Back. I knew all about them. They had caused Swift Enterprises a whole lot of trouble over the years. The Road Back claimed to be "Natural Living Activists." They said that all the necessities humankind ever needed to survive and prosper were already here on Earth, and that, by pursuing "artificial" ways of advancing ourselves, such as space travel, we were tipping the delicate balance our home planet provided for us.

That's what they *said*, at least.

In reality, they were more like "Anti-Progress Terrorists." They were so fanatical in their beliefs that they used any means necessary to derail scientific endeavors they didn't like. Sometimes those means were violent and dangerous. The worst part was that there was no reasoning with members of The Road Back. They were as devoted to their cause as any religious fanatic.

"They have been here, outside the gates of Above and Beyond, since the Apogee project was announced," Joao said. "Usually, they just wave signs and yell. I have never seen them do this!"

"It must be because the opening date is so close," I suggested.

Sandy recoiled from the face glaring at her from the other side of her window. "We're just outside the gates?! Doesn't Above and Beyond have security? Why aren't they helping us?!"

The limousine started to rock from side to side. Sandy dug her fingers into my arm. I was going to have bruises tomorrow! "We have security," Joao assured us. "But it will take time for them to reach the limousine."

"I hope there's a limousine left by the time they get here," I muttered.

Suddenly, there was a *crash!* from the window next to Sandy. She yelped and practically jumped into my lap. The glass of the window had split into a spiderweb pattern—one of these wackos had thrown a rock at it, unconcerned that he might hit one of his fellow pro-testers! This was getting serious—too serious!

"Okay, that's enough," I said, gently moving Sandy away from me so I could unzip my carry-on bag and dig through it.

"What are you doing?" Sandy demanded.

Joao turned around at her question, wanting to see what was up. "Do you have some kind of 'protester remover' in there?"

"Maybe," I said, pulling out a metal cylinder the size of a football. Attached to it were two exhaust ports mounted on swivels. From the cylinder, I unfolded two thin handles, each of which ended in grips studded with control buttons. Two canvas straps dangled down from its sides.

Sandy's eyes opened even wider. "You brought *that* with you?"

"I've been tinkering with it just for this trip," I said. It was a jetpack, one that could be worn like a backpack, thanks to the canvas straps. The cylinder was filled with tightly compressed air that could be released through the exhaust ports at the touch of the control buttons. The buttons also directed the exhaust ports so the user could control which direction he moved. I figured it would be perfect to use on the EVAs—Extra-Vehicular Activities, which is what astronauts called space walks—I hoped to take after we settled in on Apogee.

"Joao," I said, "when I say so, I want you to open the limousine's sunroof."

"Are you crazy?" Sandy yelped. "The second he does that, one of those weirdos will fall right into our lap!"

"Trust me," I said to her. I positioned the jetpack's exhaust ports so they were directly under the sunroof, pointing straight up. "Joao, are you ready?"

Joao poised his finger over a button on the limo's dashboard. He nodded. "Anytime you are saying," he said.

I nodded back. "Right now."

He pushed the button, and the sunroof began to slide open. Sandy covered her face and shrank back into her seat.

As the roof opened, I saw more protestors lying across it, blocking out the sky. One happened to have his face pointed down at the car, and our eyes met. He snarled! "Throw away technology," he yelled. "Natural life is the only life!"

"Yeah," I said, "we'll talk about it after your trip."

I pushed the "full-thrust" button on the jetpack's handle, and a powerful burst of air shot up from the exhaust ports and into the protester's stomach.

"Boof," he managed to say as the wind was knocked out of him. He shot up into the air as though flung from a catapult, arching over and away from the limousine.

The heads of the other protestors crowding the car whipped around to follow their colleague's path. Then panic set in, and they ran screaming from the limo before whatever was inside could do to them what it had done to their friend!

The path between us and the gate to the Above and Beyond compound was momentarily clear. Joao floored the gas, and the limousine lurched forward with a screech. The gate opened, we veered through, and it closed again behind us, just as the protestors were recovering their wits. I swung around to look out the back window and saw the poor guy I had blasted, limping back up to the front ranks, holding his stomach in pain but shouting passionately through the bars of the gate. He'd feel that compressed air burst for a while, but he'd be fine.

"Remind me never to make fun of your gizmos again," Sandy said, sounding relieved.

"Yeah, knowing you, you'll probably hold off on teasing me for a whole two days," I cracked.

Up in front, I could hear Joao speaking under his

breath, but my Portuguese wasn't good enough for me to make out what he was saying. "What's that, Joao?" I asked.

"I was just saying thank you," he said quietly, pointing to the roof of the limo. It took me a second to realize he meant he was thanking the heavens. "And thank you, too. That item of yours comes in very dandy, I think."

I laughed. "Handy," I corrected him. "It comes in handy."

"It's pretty dandy, too, if you ask me," Sandy added.

"We are here," Joao announced, swinging the limo into the circular driveway of a long, flat building sandwiched between two taller buildings. "Welcome, finally, to Above and Beyond!"

4

The Launch Lobby

I looked around, squinting at the sunlight coming in through the now-clear car windows. In big letters over the building's entrance were the words ABOVE AND BEYOND. It looked like an immense industrial park, except that it stood alone in the middle of a great big span of empty land. There literally wasn't another building or sign of civilization as far as the eye could see. How the protestors got out here, and where they went when the day was done, I had no idea. Maybe they slept right outside the gate!

We climbed out of the car, and I stretched my arm way over my head, trying to get my blood to circulate once more. "Don't tell me you're still sleepy after all that excitement," Sandy said.

"Hardly," I assured her with a smile. "My arm's just cranky from sleeping on it."

As Joao unloaded our bags from the trunk, I saw the doors of the building before us slide open and a middle-aged woman come charging out, a big smile on her face. She was dressed in the craziest outfit I'd ever seen—it looked like every part of her wardrobe came from a different part of the planet! On her head, covering her bright red hair, she wore a crocheted tam that probably came from somewhere in the Caribbean. She had on a khaki vest emblazoned with patches of a hundred different countries, over a large, loose shirt I recognized as an Egyptian *galabiyah*. She wore traditional wooden shoes that must have come from Holland—they made a *clop-clop* sound as she walked across the sidewalk. And she wore good old American blue jeans.

"Tom and Sandy Swift," she squawked, reaching us and standing with her hands on her hips. "It's about time our celebrities got here! Now maybe we can get on our way to Apogee! I'm Elaine Kaufman, senior writer for *Global Vista* travel magazine!" She thrust out her hand to me, but I was still stunned by her garb, so I hesitated a moment. Joao jumped in and grabbed her hand, pumping it enthusiastically.

"I'm Joao," he told her, his gold tooth flashing as he smiled. "I am the driver of the celebrities!"

Elaine half smiled, half glared at him, and dropped her hand. Joao took our bags into the building, and Elaine put an arm around both my sister's shoulder and mine and steered us to the entrance. "I had to beg, borrow, and steal to get this assignment," she informed us. "The chance to be the first reviewer of a space hotel? You bet I wanted the job! And I know I'm only along to help bring a little publicity to this interstellar spa, but trust me: I'm going to review it like I would any other place! If the room service stinks, I'm writing about it!"

In that case, I thought, *the room service better not stink.* After all Swift Enterprises had put into Apogee, the space hotel needed to be a success.

The doors to the Above and Beyond Launch Lobby whooshed open, and we stepped inside. The reception area was enormous, and its entire back wall was made of glass, allowing us to look out at the launchpad well in the distance. There, standing upright and attached to massive booster rockets, stood a Swift Enterprises shuttle, which would soon be taking us into outer space. It was an impressive sight, standing tall and strong against the flat, empty backdrop. With nothing to distract from it, it literally commanded your attention. I had watched plenty of launches on television before, and I'd even attended the launching of a few Swift rockets, but knowing I was actually going to *be* on that craft added a whole new level of thrill.

There weren't many people in the Lobby, which had corridors left and right that led into the other buildings in the complex. There were just a few Above and Beyond staffers in sky-blue jumpsuits, and a few other civilians like Sandy, Elaine, and me. I noticed an older woman standing with a boy about my age, and a thin, meek-looking man standing off by himself. Elaine led us in their direction, and they turned from the glass window as we approached.

"Kids, meet our roommates," Elaine said. "Well, our *hotel* mates. At least for the next few days, right?"

She pointed to the older woman. "Tom and Sandy Swift, this is Victoria Fogarty."

Sandy gaped. "From Fogarty Cosmetics? The fourth-richest woman in the world?"

"Third," Ms. Fogarty said dismissively. "Although I *could* drop to fourth, depending on how much this little trip costs me. But I've always wanted to see outer space, so I'm sure it'll be worth it."

Her son snorted. "If it's not, maybe you can buy outer space and fix it up so you like it more."

I turned to the boy, who was a little shorter than me but a lot more muscular. He had muscles on top of his muscles. His face seemed to be fixed in a permanent scowl, his eyebrows scrunched together. "Hey," I said, "I'm Tom."

"'S'up," he grunted.

"Brendan, be nice," his mother scolded. "You were worried there weren't going to be any people your age on this trip!"

Brendan shrugged and turned back to the window. I looked to his mother, who was at least a little more friendly. "Ms. Fogarty, your family isn't related in any way to the Foger Utility Group, are you? Your names are kinda similar. . . ."

She thought about it for a moment, tapping her finger against her chin. "I don't really know. It's entirely possible we own stock in them—or perhaps we even *own* them—but I've never looked at our entire list of holdings. I should really do that sometime."

Elaine cleared her throat and turned to the skinny man. He was rail thin, and looked like he might snap in half if a good wind came up. He was balding and wore spectacles. He had an absentminded look on his face, but his eyes twinkled. I figured there was a lot going on in that head of his. "And this is Dr. Peter Gorinsky," she told us. "He's making a rare trip out of his lab in North Dakota to see what outer space is all about."

"I read a lot of articles you wrote when I was researching Apogee," I told him excitedly. "You've been a big supporter of space tourism for a long time!"

He looked away from me as he talked, as though embarrassed. "Yes, well, it's going to be a broad market for tourists, and the benefits to world economies have enormous potential. . . ."

Ms. Fogarty squinted at him. "You know, I met a Peter Gorinsky at an aerospace conference in Washington . . . oh, it must have been twelve years ago!"

Dr. Gorinsky blushed, unable or unwilling to look at her either. "It's quite possible," he mumbled. "I've been to so many conferences, met so many people. . . . It's part of why I retreated to my lab. Shaking hands was taking too much time away from my research."

"Didn't you have a beard back then?" she asked.

"Oh, uh, I've had a beard at several times in my life," he stammered, clearly uncomfortable. "It's quite difficult for me to remember when I've had one and when I haven't. I hope you understand." He said the last sentence in such a way that I could tell he was hoping this would be the end of the conversation.

Ms. Fogarty looked like she was about to ask more questions, anyway, but a deep voice spoke from behind us. "Hi, folks! Everybody ready for a little trip to outer space?"

We turned and saw a massive bear of a man in a powder-blue suit that matched the jumpsuits the staffers wore. On his lapel was a sparkling metal pin molded in the Apogee logo. He had a ruddy complexion, with thinning red hair, but a long, bushy beard. His brown eyes glowed with kindness and energy.

"Hi, Uncle Giles!" Sandy exclaimed, surprising him with a hug.

Giles Burton practically *was* an uncle to Sandy and me; we had known him all our lives. He'd been our father's roommate in college—they'd stayed up almost every night talking excitedly about the plans they had for making the world a better place through science. While my dad went on to explore a wide range of scientific interests, Giles had decided to focus exclusively on astrophysics and microgravity engineering and architecture. He founded Above and

Beyond and had devoted his entire adult life to it, never slowing down to marry or have kids of his own. "Above and Beyond *is* my kid," he had said many times. And the company had come a long way, providing designs and technical support for the International Space Station, as well as creating long-range probes that were headed out of the Milky Way to study other galaxies and report back. Apogee, though, was to be the company's first real moment in the sun. Conceived and built from Giles's plans, it was literally his life's work. If successful, Apogee would mark Above and Beyond as *the* name in space technology and research.

He laughed and hugged Sandy back, one massive hand practically covering her entire back. "Hello, Bug," he said, using the nickname he'd had for her since she was a baby.

I stuck out my hand. "Hi, Giles," I said.

He put his hands on his hips in mock indignation. "Ho, too big and adult to give me a hug? Forget that!"

He reached out and grabbed me, pulling me into his chest and squeezing me tight. I heard him laugh, the vibrations passing through his sternum into my skull, and I wanted to laugh too, but the truth was, I couldn't breathe. When he let me go, I felt a little dizzy. It was a good kind of dizzy, though.

Giles turned to the rest of his guests and smiled warmly. "You'll excuse me if I don't hug all of you," he said. "I've known these pups for a while, so they get a bit more of a hello than most folks."

Dr. Gorinsky looked at him with a little distaste. "Quite all right, I'm sure."

"Well, I don't see any more reason to waste time," Giles said. "I've waited years for this launch, so let's get on with it! Based on the measurements you sent us, we've got your custom-made space suits ready to go. Feel like trying them on? Follow me."

I didn't need to be asked twice! Sandy and I, along with the others, hurried after him.

But before I took more than a few steps, I felt a hand on my arm. I turned, and so did Sandy. It was Joao, looking at us with fond smiles. Suddenly, I felt embarrassed and reached into my pocket. "I'm so stupid! Sorry, Joao . . . We forgot to tip you!"

Joao shook his head. "No, no. No tip necessary," he assured us. "Your father already sent along a tip for me. Very generous man! No, I want to give you a going-away gift!"

"You don't have to do that, Joao," Sandy said.

"We're just glad we had the chance to meet you."

Our driver shook his head again. "No, no. This gift is necessary. No one should travel without it!"

"If you mean a toothbrush," I joked, "I'm pretty sure I packed mine."

He reached under the collar of his Hawaiian shirt and lifted a thin chain from around his neck. At the end of it dangled a small medallion. He cupped it in his hand and held it out to us, showing us the Portuguese inscription. "It is a Brazilian poem to protect travelers. You take it. Just in case."

"Joao, that's really nice," I said, waving my hands in front of me, "but we can't take something as personal as that!"

"Pfff," he said, dismissing me. "This medallion is what protected us on the drive here!"

He put the chain in my hand. "Are you sure?" I asked him.

He nodded firmly. "Very sure. It would be bad if you needed it and didn't have it, right?"

It was hard to argue with that!

"Just give it back to me when you get home!" he insisted, pointing at me seriously.

"We will, we will," I promised, laughing.

He grabbed our hands, giving them vigorous farewell shakes. "Safe journey," he said, then walked the other way without looking back.

"Come on," Sandy said, tugging at my sleeve. "We have to catch up to the others!"

I followed her, looking down at the medallion in my hand, suddenly a little uneasy. Did Joao think there was some reason we *needed* protection on our trip? I sure hoped not.

We rejoined our fellow travelers as they walked through the long corridor to one of the buildings attached to the reception area. We worked our way past the Fogartys and Dr. Gorinsky to Giles, who was busy answering rapid fire questions from Elaine Kaufman.

"How many inflatable modules can Apogee accommodate?"

"Currently, we're set up for sixteen, and that's how many we have operating. But theoretically, there's no limit. We can attach modules to modules, and more modules to those. Because we have unlimited space, we're only limited by our imagination and ambition!"

"What about air? Cooling and heating?"

Giles was about to answer, but Sandy jumped in.

"There are three recyclers aboard Apogee, with enough filters in store to last three months. Regular resupply shuttles will bring more on a regular schedule. Each room and common area has its own thermostat, like any other hotel."

Giles and Ms. Kaufman stared at her in surprise. Sandy shrugged. "I've been studying the hotel's specs."

"You mean you have them memorized," I teased her. Sandy never learned anything halfway. She committed everything to her memory, and so far, there didn't seem to be a limit to how much it could hold.

The travel reporter dropped back, making notes on her small pad, and we continued to follow Giles, practically running to keep up with his long stride.

"How's your father doing with that radiation-shielding project?" he asked.

"It's coming along," I told him. "I just wish they hadn't given him such a short deadline."

Giles snorted. "They're *always* short deadlines," he said.

"He really wanted to be here," said Sandy. "He knows how much this means to you."

"I know," Giles replied with a kindly smile. "He'd be here if he could. But you're here, and that's just as good!"

We hurried on, and I tucked Joao's medallion into my pocket, making a mental note to make sure I put it somewhere in my space suit. After all, it couldn't hurt!

Twenty minutes later, I was sitting in my space suit, wearing everything but the gloves and the helmet. The suit was much lighter and less bulky than the normal space suits astronauts wore, thanks to Above and Beyond's research into a new fabric that was not only temperature resistant (I didn't even get warm wearing it) but close to puncture proof. . . . The suit no longer needed to have multiple layers to protect the wearer against a puncture that might cause a loss in oxygen supply.

I was checking again to make sure my jetpack was in good condition when Sandy sat down next to me. "Did you pack your Swift Speak?" I asked her.

"Sure," she answered. "It doesn't take up much room at all. Why?"

"Because I want to be able to talk to you while I'm spacewalking!"

"Gee," she said, wrinkling her brow, "are you sure you know how to spacewalk and talk at the same time?"

I gave her a playful shove. "Ho, ho," I said. "*Now who's being funny?*"

Giles returned to the room and smiled again. "Everyone comfortable in their suits? Great! Because the launch clock has started, and we're two hours away from liftoff. Time to head to the shuttle!"

I grabbed my helmet and gloves, so excited that I was ready to race out the door even ahead of the project's creator! But Giles put his hands on both Sandy's and my shoulders and gently held us back. He kneeled down to look us in the eyes. "Have a good trip, kids," he said softly.

"Thanks, Uncle Giles," Sandy replied. "Thanks for letting us go up there."

He nodded, then said, "Don't let anything happen to my baby." He was smiling when he said it, but I could hear the nervousness in his voice, barely there, deep in the background. Finally, he let us go and we started walking away. I looked back over my shoulder at him as he stood up and sighed. The next few days would mean everything to him. I reached into my pocket and touched Joao's medallion, hoping it wouldn't just bring Sandy and me good luck, but Giles as well.

5

The Second Wild Ride

"Solid rocket booster ignition and liftoff!"

The voice crackled over my helmet radio, and I was surprised I could hear it. I expected to hear the thunderous roar of the liquid fuel booster rockets, but the shuttle was so well insulated that, aside from the shaking and vibrating of the cabin, I wouldn't have even known that we were taking off.

Sandwiched between Sandy and Brendan Fogarty in my flight chair, lying on my back with my feet up in the air, I didn't have a window to look out of, but there was a monitor before me on the instrument console. Its image currently showed the view from a camera attached to one of the external tanks and pointed down at the ground. I watched with amazement as it receded farther and farther beneath us, covered in the billowing smoke from our engines. A moment later, Earth had been reduced to a series of farmland grids, thin roads with cars turned into slow-moving dots, and the occasional cluster of buildings and activity that signified a small town or village.

It didn't feel any different—at least not so far—from taking off in a regular airplane.

Which isn't to say the takeoff was smooth. The shaking was pretty violent, like we were in a car driving over a cobblestone road. I wasn't scared—I had done plenty of reading on what to expect when taking off on a space flight—but I was a little nervous. How could I not be? It wasn't like I was hopping on my bike and just riding down to the corner store for a carton of milk.

"Yahoo!" Sandy yelled enthusiastically, her voice faint through my helmet. Apparently she wasn't even nervous.

There was a faint *clank* as the empty booster casings fell away from the craft, and the ride smoothed out considerably. Because the shuttle was lighter now, we could feel our speed increase, and the force of gravity, magnified, squashed me back into my padded seat. Even breathing became difficult. It's definitely a weird experience to feel your face flattening out as three times the regular force of gravity presses down on it! Luckily, my time in the "Vomit Comet" had prepared me well.

"We have MECO," said the voice in my helmet after maybe five minutes of acceleration.

Main Engines Cutoff. The thrust from the engines pulled back to zero in just a matter of seconds, and the weight disappeared from my chest. I could feel the pressure from the restraint straps holding me in place against the chair, and I could feel my suit where it touched my skin, but otherwise, I knew I was now weightless. The monitor now showed the view from another camera, this one attached to the body of the shuttle itself. It wasn't pointed at Earth, but rather ahead. . . . All it showed was inky blackness, peppered with random stars. It was one thing to read about and study for a ride like this, but it was another thing to actually find myself way up here, in orbit around Earth! I just gaped at the monitor, stunned.

"Out of this world," I said spacily.

The trip to Apogee took several hours, but as this was the first such flight to the hotel, the passengers were asked not to unbuckle themselves and float freely around the cabin. It was a cautious atmosphere—the pilots wanted to double- and triple-check that they were doing everything right, and they didn't want the distraction of cheery space tourists literally bouncing off the walls!

"What a rip," Brendan growled. "What's the point of being on a spaceship if you can't have any fun while you're on it?"

"Brendan, dear, relax," his mother, Victoria, said. "Once we're on Apogee, you'll practically have the entire place to yourself. We'll be the only guests! You can romp around all you like!"

"All by myself, great," Brendan muttered. "I don't see why you couldn't arrange for one of my friends to come. It's not like we can't afford it. . . ."

"It's not a matter of money, Brendan. . . . The hotel is only prepared to accommodate a certain number of people for its initial trial run."

Brendan jerked a thumb across my chest at Sandy. "Why did *she* have to come? She's so young, it's not like she's going to get anything out of it!"

"*What* did he say?" Sandy asked, trying to lean over me to glare at Brendan.

"Nothing," I said quickly. I stuck my arm out, forcing Sandy to lean back into her seat. I wanted to defuse any tension as fast as I could, mostly because I knew that if Brendan kept after my sister, I might get really upset. But what I was *really* worried about was that *Sandy* would get upset . . . and, believe me, that wouldn't be pretty for Brendan! So I made nice. "I'll hang out with you, Brendan," I said as cheerily as I could manage. "We'll have a blast."

"There, now," Ms. Fogarty said soothingly. "Isn't that nice? You'll have a *blast*."

Brendan rolled his eyes.

The voice inside my helmet was back. "Stand by for docking in fifteen seconds."

I quickly shifted my eyes to the external camera. I'd been so busy playing peacemaker that I hadn't even noticed we were practically on top of Apogee. We were too close for me to see the entire hotel, so all I could see was the approaching dock set into the smooth center column of the structure. I felt goose bumps rise on my skin. I couldn't wait to set foot— or, more accurately, to *float*—on Apogee.

Except, I reminded myself, *now you're going to be stuck*

with Frown-Face Fogarty for the entire trip. Smooth move, Swift!

With a gentle bump, the shuttle came to a stop and we heard a quiet, solid *click*—the craft locking into the docking bay. There was a soft *hiss* as the air pressure in the shuttle changed just slightly, to match the pressure inside Apogee.

"Okay," said the pilot over our helmet microphones. "Here's the moment you've all been waiting for—feel free to get up and move around as you like."

We unbuckled ourselves from our seats and gently floated off of them in the microgravity. I kept expecting it to end, for us to regain our weight and be crushed back into the chairs—I was used to experiencing the sensation aboard the "Vomit Comet." But this was the real thing! Unless we wanted to be anchored up here, we could float freely as much as we wanted.

I could fly!

Everyone started using the handholds and footholds to propel themselves to the air lock, which would soon open, allowing us entrance to the hotel. Dr. Gorinsky couldn't seem to get his bearings, I noticed, grabbing rather wildly for things and sending himself tumbling awkwardly. I couldn't help but laugh.

"I thought you'd been in space a bunch of times, Dr. Gorinsky! I figured you'd be used to microgravity by now!"

"Some people *never* get used to it," he moaned. Then he sniffled. "Worse, every time I come up here, my sinuses plug up!"

Miserable, he managed to maneuver himself past me. I felt bad for laughing. Clogged sinuses was a common complaint for astronauts. It definitely wasn't fatal, but it wasn't fun, either. Not everyone was going to have as good a time as I was.

We gathered near the air lock, waiting for the door to open from the other side. I could barely contain myself! In just seconds I was going to be one of the first people—*ever!*—to set foot inside the first space hotel in history!

There was a *thunk-clunk* of lock mechanisms turning and releasing, and then the door swung open. I don't know what I was expecting to see—something out of a science fiction movie, maybe, with high-tech, futuristic lighting, lots of computer display panels and equipment.

Instead, I saw what looked like a normal hallway in a very nice hotel: plush carpeting, evenly spaced light fixtures along the walls (using plain old light-bulbs, it seemed), colorful art hanging in subdued frames, and wood-paneled doors. Nothing about the place seemed the least bit out of the ordinary—it was as though we were stepping into a hotel in New York, or Paris, or Sydney.

No, there was nothing unusual whatsoever . . . except for the man who greeted us. Don't get me wrong; he had both eyes, his ears were in the right places, and he smiled perfectly pleasantly.

But he was standing on the ceiling.

"Hi everyone," he said. "I'm David Wong, the hotel manager. Welcome to Apogee!"

Apogee

I liked David Wong right away. He had a friendly smile and a way of talking that let you know that, while he liked to kid around by doing such things as standing on the ceiling, he took his job very seriously.

He wore a black suit and a black tie, but on his feet he wore what looked like white slippers. As he stepped off the ceiling and onto the wall, then down onto the floor so he could face us, he explained, "Sorry for the unorthodox way of greeting you folks, but I wanted to welcome you in a way that could only be done on Apogee, and this seemed like the best way to do it!"

He lifted up one of his feet and showed us the bottom of his slippers, which were striped with what looked like Velcro. "These slippers and the walls of the hotel—not to mention most of the pieces of individual furniture in the guest rooms—are lined with adhesive material so you can maneuver on all surfaces of any room," he said. Then, pointing to a row of slippers on the floor near our feet, he continued, "We have a set of slippers for each of you. Feel free to take a few minutes to get adjusted."

We each took off our space suit boots and slid our feet into the slippers. They made a quiet crackle when lifted off the surface of the air-lock floor. Moving in them was relatively easy, a little like walking across the surface of a theater floor after soda has been spilled on it. Excited to give it a try, I quickly walked up the wall to stand on the ceiling. I looked down at David Wong as he continued. Then I noticed a bunch of small robots scuttling about in the corridors beyond the docking bay, moving back and forth on small tracks set into the flooring and walls. I wanted to ask David about them, but he was still delivering his "welcome" speech. "We've oriented furniture and fixtures in most of the hotel's common areas, like the hallways, meeting rooms, and lobby, so there's a recognizable 'floor.'"

Sandy maneuvered herself onto the wall to David's left. "What about beds? Are they stuck to the floors too?"

"Easy, kid," Elaine Kaufman cracked. "Questions like that are my job!"

David laughed easily. "I'll answer all your questions, I promise," he said. "While your bags are being taken to your rooms, how about a little tour?"

"Yes, please," Sandy and Ms. Kaufman exclaimed at the same time. They looked at each other in comical shock, and then all of us broke into laughter—except Brendan, of course. And Dr. Gorinsky, who only sniffled.

"Excellent," David said, clapping his hands together. "Then follow me . . . on any wall or ceiling you'd like!"

For the first part of the tour, I stayed on the ceiling, but as everything was set on the "floor," I got a little dizzy after a while and had to come down to the same level on which David walked. The walls and floor were all slightly spongy, like the mats of a martial arts studio. I figured that after a while I'd become used to walking around upside down or perpendicular to the floor—at least I hoped so. It would sure be a shame to come all this way and not be able to take advantage of one of the cooler parts of the space hotel experience.

As we maneuvered through the corridors, Ms. Kaufman peppered David with questions so sharp, they almost sounded like ones you might hear at a police interrogation. "What qualifies someone to be a space hotel manager, Mr. Wong? It's not a job anyone's ever had before. . . . How could anyone possibly be prepared for something like this?"

"Please, Ms. Kaufman," he replied, "it's David. And I guess I was a pretty obvious choice for the job. I was an astronaut for NASA, and I've logged more time on international space stations and shuttles than any man alive. My body's very conditioned to life in microgravity, and I feel more at home up here than down on Earth, so when my commitment to the navy was up and I heard about the Apogee project, I applied immediately. A few courses in hotel management, and here I am!"

"Do you have enough of a crew to run this station?

I haven't seen another person since we got here," Ms. Kaufman said.

"Well, much of the station is automated," he told her, then pointed out a tall, column-shaped robot approaching us on a central track in the floor. It was bigger than the small ones I'd seen before—taller and a little broader than an average human—but most of its body was storage: The robot had a large, hollow chest cavity behind a Plexiglas door. It looked like I was finally going to get my explanation as to what these robots actually did! The robot, sensing the obstruction in front of it, stopped and beeped politely, blue light flickering from a dorsal antenna, as though asking for permission to pass. We stepped aside, and it rolled past us to the door to the next air lock. "Robots like these handle most of the chores aboard Apogee, such as cooking and housecleaning. They're a lot more efficient—and inexpensive—than maintaining a human staff." We watched as a panel slid open in the robot's side and a long, skinny arm ending in a key card, like the kind you'd find in any normal Earthside hotel, extended to the door's lock. The key card was inserted and retracted, and the door slid up. The robot passed through, and a smaller robot, exactly like the one I'd seen before, crossed in front of it. They traded beeps and boops, their antennas alight, then the smaller one slid aside so the larger could pass. Once it did, the little robot moved toward, then past us through another air lock. The door came down once again.

"Most of our robots are that size," David said, pointing to the smaller robot as it skittered past. "We call them all 'Jeeves.' You'll see a lot of them. They communicate with one another like an ant colony, each member aware of what each other member has to do. Again, efficiency.

"Once we're fully operational," he went on, "we'll have around sixty full-time human staff, most of them technicians, and many of them former astronauts. During your stay, we're working with a skeleton crew, so you'll probably only see ten or twelve other people aboard."

"What happens if someone gets sick up here? How do you expect to handle that?" the travel reporter asked.

"Good question. The answer is the first stop on our tour." David inserted his own key card into a door lock, and the door obligingly lifted to reveal the hotel's infirmary.

It was a large room with a tall ceiling. Instead of hospital beds, there were about thirty sleeping bags, very cushioned and thick, anchored to three of the walls at various levels heading up to the ceiling. Near each was a complete set of health monitors and anchors for any necessary medical equipment. On the fourth wall, also at differing levels leading to the ceiling, were different medical "stations": a small X-ray machine; a lab with centrifuges and beakers; a long, locked cabinet filled with medications; and several others. "We're not equipped for major surgery here on Apogee," David admitted, "but we can set a broken bone, accommodate an allergy attack, and even treat an outbreak of space-sickness."

"Can you do anything for my sinuses?" Dr. Gorinsky asked, sounding even more congested than before. He was getting worse in a hurry.

"We have standard decongestants," David told him. "We'll be happy to give you a nasal spray." Dr. Gorinsky nodded, looking relieved.

"In the case of pretty much anything more serious than the minor things I mentioned," David went on, "we can stabilize a patient until he or she can be shuttled back to Earth. We've got two medical technicians currently onboard, and when we have a full complement of guests, we'll have a med staff of nine."

Dr. Gorinsky detached his feet from the floor and floated up to inspect the various medical stations. "Remarkable," he said, examining a sleeping bag. "I assume these are your . . . 'hospital beds'?"

"That's right." David nodded, floating up to join him. "They're lined with sensors so we can keep current on all of a patient's vital signs. They're firmly anchored so they can't bang against the walls under any circumstances. Similar sleeping bags can be found in the guest rooms, only without all the sensors, of course."

"Remarkable," Dr. Gorinsky said again.

As we left the room, David sidled over to Sandy and me. "How are you guys doing?" he wanted to know. "I'm glad you were able to make it. Sorry your dad couldn't be here."

"This is a great place, Mr. Wong," Sandy enthused, and I had to nod in agreement. It sure was.

"Hey, what goes for Ms. Kaufman goes for you, too, Sandy," David said, shaking his head in mock sternness. "Call me David."

"I have about a million questions for you, David," I blurted, so excited, I couldn't keep from talking a mile a minute. "I want to hear all about your experiences in space, all the missions—everything!"

He laughed. "Well, I'm going to be pretty busy while you're here, making sure all the hotel's systems are working smoothly, but I'm sure we'll have some time to get together and chat."

Victoria Fogarty had stopped in front of a door marked RESTRICTED ACCESS. "What's in here?" she wanted to know.

"That's our Command Center," David replied. "There are several entry points to it, from important departments on the facility, as well as a few of the corridors. It's really the hub of everything we do. I'm only sorry we can't show it to you."

Elaine Kaufman raised her eyebrows. "Why not? Are you trying to hide something?"

"Of course not," David answered, a little indignantly. I could tell he was starting to get annoyed with her questions, and I couldn't blame him. "Our Control Room is off-limits for security reasons. As you may know, Apogee has already been condemned by The Road Back, and we take such matters very seriously."

"We know all about how The Road Back feels about the hotel," Sandy said sourly. "They told us personally."

David nodded grimly. "I'd heard about the demonstrations. I guess they're becoming more belligerent?"

"That's a kind word," Ms. Kaufman replied.

David sighed and shook his head before returning to the tour. "In any event, the central core of the hotel, which we're in now, is made up primarily of the Control Room and the infirmary," he said, moving to another door. "The guest facilities, as you know, are located in the inflatable modules ringing the core." He used another key card, and a door lifted, leading us into an air lock between the core and a guest wing, like we'd seen the robot use earlier.

Coming out the other side of the air lock, into the corridor of a guest module, we found another long hallway, with a designated "floor" and several doors branching off of it.

David used his key card to lead us into another room, this one outfitted with several small viewports as well as anchored tables and chairs that slid a foot back from those tables on small tracks. Panels in the walls offered various food items, several of them—

and all of the beverages—in tubes, like astronauts had used for decades. "While there's certainly room service available if guests want it, each module features a dining area like this one. There's even daily specials!"

In the next room, we saw pieces of gymnastic equipment, like parallel bars and rings, anchored to the walls at all levels. Across the floor was an array of stationary bicycles. "Traditional free weights and treadmills don't mean a whole lot in microgravity," David said. "But guests wanting a good workout can find a mini-gym in each module."

Brendan elbowed me. "We'll have to do some racing on those bikes, huh, Swift?"

"Uh, sure," I said, startled. It was the first thing Brendan had said to anyone that wasn't angry, a grunt—or both!

"What about showers?" Elaine asked. "After a good workout, you're likely to be pretty sweaty, right?"

David nodded. "It's true. Unfortunately, typical showers and baths aren't the most useful up here. But we're well stocked with larger versions of the moist towelettes you might use to wipe your hands before a meal, and those do a pretty good job. We've even got a special solution that works like shampoo."

Next up was sort of a microgravity rec room. In cabinets and containers along the wall were pieces of sporting equipment and toys. The main area of the chamber was wide open and well padded. "For younger guests, as well as those who simply want to have a little physical fun, these 'game rooms' have just about everything they could ask for," David said, smiling. "Let me tell you, microgravity basketball is pretty different from the traditional game . . . and, if you ask me, a lot more fun!"

David stopped before the last door and turned to us dramatically. "Last stop on our tour, folks," he said. "Prepare yourself for the best part of Apogee."

He used his key card, the door slid up . . . and I saw the most amazing sight I'd ever seen in my entire life! There, before us, was a giant porthole of sorts, a massive window looking out of the space station at the vast, inky blackness of space! Below us and to the left was the blue-green curve of Earth. I could make out India, a large, swirled pattern of clouds hanging over its southern tip. To either side of us I could see portions of the inflatable modules connected to ours—they looked like balloons, or marshmallows. And above us was the moon, ghostly white and bigger than I'd ever seen it. From here, craters and indentations could be seen plainly, and it glowed powerfully.

Everyone was stunned into silence. Except Brendan. "Big deal," Brendan muttered. "Looks like any picture you can find on the NASA website."

"Yeah, but you're seeing it for real!" Sandy exclaimed, sounding like she couldn't believe that Brendan could blow off something so majestic. "This is totally incredible!" But Brendan only shrugged. Apparently, nothing impressed him . . . except the gym.

"We figure the view is going to be one of the main drawing points of a hotel like Apogee," David said, a hint of a smile in his voice. "So we've maximized viewing portals—with large community ones in each module entrance, and another in every guest room."

"Isn't it magnificent, Dr. Gorinsky?" Victoria Fogarty asked. "Just like that man described it at that aerospace conference! What was his name? Brewster? Brewer? Sutter?"

"I'm quite sure I don't remember," Dr. Gorinsky said, looking very uncomfortable.

"Oh, you must," Ms. Fogarty insisted. "He was very tall, and had such a thick, white beard! I can't believe I don't remember his name—he was positively unforgettable! Cloomer? Clooney? Rooney?"

"I-I-" Dr. Gorinsky stammered, then put a hand to the side of his head. "I'm afraid I'm not feeling very well," he said in a pinched voice.

"Space-sickness on top of your clogged sinuses—that can't be a lot of fun," David said. Then, noticing Elaine Kaufman making notes at this diagnosis, he hastily added, "It doesn't have anything to do with the hotel, but rather the individual affected. Much like the sinus problems, some people simply get it, others don't." He thumbed a button on a remote he took from his pocket, and a small robot zipped up to us, beeping accommodatingly. "Jeeves will show you the way back to the infirmary, and one of our medical techs will be happy to take care of you."

Dr. Gorinsky nodded and followed the small robot back through the corridors. A moment later, five more robots of the same size appeared. "It looks like your bellboys are here, everyone," David said. "They'll take you to your rooms, where you'll find your bags and key cards. If you need anything, don't hesitate to call!"

Sandy looked up at me, her eyes wide. "We get our own rooms?!"

"I guess so," I said, shrugging. "Why, are you thinking about throwing a big party?"

She socked me in the arm. "Ha-ha," she said. "I'm just glad I don't have to be around the mess you always make, clothes and stuff everywhere!"

"Just for that, I think I'll take you back to that rec room and kick your butt at microgravity badminton," I said, challenging her.

"You *wish* you could beat me," she replied, taking the bait.

Reluctantly, I turned to Brendan. "You want to come play with us, Brendan?"

He chuckled. "Badminton? I don't think so. After I check out my room, I'm going back to the gym to work out!"

"Can we go to the rec room instead of our rooms?" Sandy asked the robots. They beeped in unison, apparently saying yes.

As we started to leave, I turned back to Elaine

Kaufman, who was settling into a plush chair in front of the viewport. "Want to come watch us, Ms. Kaufman?"

"No thanks, Tom," she called back. "I think I'm going to stay here and make some notes for my story."

"You're not going to miss much," Sandy said with a mischievous grin. "Just me humiliating Tom!"

I grabbed my sister in a playful headlock and mussed her hair. "*Now* who's dreaming?"

Laughing, we followed the small robots.

Restricted Access

"Game point," Sandy said, readying herself to serve.

I braced myself to return. I'd thought it would be easy to beat Sandy at microgravity badminton, but boy, had I been wrong.

We'd taken off our slippers to float freely in the room, and setting up the net had been easy enough—just anchoring it to loops drilled into opposing walls—but playing had been another matter entirely. I'd tossed the shuttlecock into the air, waiting for it to come down so I could serve it, just like in a game of regular badminton played in the backyard. Only the shuttlecock hadn't come down. Without gravity to pull it toward the floor, it just kept going up, up, up, until it struck the ceiling and lazily drifted off to one side.

I retrieved it by grabbing a handhold on the wall and pulling myself up to its level, then tried another tack: I held the shuttlecock above my head with one hand and swung my racket overhand with the other.

Not only did I miss the shuttlecock entirely, my momentum carried me around in a free-floating somersault . . . and then another . . . and then another. I could hear Sandy laughing at me. That lasted until she tried to serve, holding the shuttlecock out in front of her and swinging her racket at it under-handed. She hit the "birdie," but it went flying straight back up to the ceiling—and Sandy was left twirling in backward somersaults!

It had been a very long game.

But, little by little, we'd figured out a way to make it work, and sort of invented our own rules. Since there was no way to make the shuttlecock arc over the net and back down, we decided to skip the net entirely and just bat the birdie back and forth between us. If you managed to get it past the other person, you got a point. Hitting the birdie wasn't so big a problem—maintaining body position was. We were still awkward, floating around, but we were getting the hang of it.

Sandy released the shuttlecock, and it hung still in front of her. She swung her racket, being careful to counter the motion with the other parts of her body so she didn't flip or spin. The birdie took off like a rocket, coming straight at me.

Concentrating hard, I sent it back to her. We volleyed like this for several shots. The score was tied, and neither of us wanted to lose. We're competitive that way, although we don't let it get out of hand.

Finally, Sandy tried a new maneuver—she banked the shuttlecock off the wall of the rec room. I was so surprised to find the birdie coming from a different angle that I swung wildly, missed, and went spinning across the room, getting tangled in the forgotten net. Sandy giggled, and even I had to laugh at this unexpected development.

"Nice shot," I managed to say.

"Just decided to think outside the box a little," she said with a shrug.

I unwrapped myself from the net, reached for a handhold, and pulled myself down to the ground. Sandy followed, and soon we were both back in our slippers, anchored to the ground. "Yeah, but now that I know the trick, our next game's gonna be a lot more interesting," I warned her.

"Whatever," she replied confidently, smiling. "I'll have thought up some *new* tricks by then!"

We exited the rec room, into one of Apogee's long corridors. "I'm going to get a snack before dinner," I said. "Want to come with me?"

Sandy shook her head. "I want to check out my room, then maybe go back to that observation deck."

"Okay. I'll catch up to you later."

She walked away down the hall in one direction, and I went the other, my feet making soft *shrrip, shrrip* noises as they pulled away from the floor. Robots scuttled madly about my feet, moving in every direction, hurrying about their duties.

I looked at the doors that I passed, trying to get my bearings. I was pretty sure I was headed in the right direction, but it was hard to tell. The corridors all looked alike, and the hotel was almost eerily silent, with no sounds to tell you what was happening where. It was a calm, almost dream-like place, but I found myself hoping Elaine Kaufman hadn't also found the hotel hard to navigate—it seemed like just the kind of thing she'd slam the hotel for in a negative review.

No sooner had I finished my thought about Ms. Kaufman than I turned another corner and saw her at the end of the next hall. She was bent in front of a door, looking at its lock mechanism with great concentration, inserting her key card into it again and again, but the door wouldn't rise. I hung back for a few moments, watching her try several more times, turning the card this way and that without success, then pushing on the door. Finally, my curiosity got the better of me, and I started down the hall toward her.

Ms. Kaufman heard the sound of my slippers approaching, and stood up in a hurry, as though she were embarrassed—like she'd been caught sneaking a cookie when everyone knew she was on a diet. "Oh hi, Tom," she stammered.

"Hey, Ms. Kaufman," I said as casually as I could. "How's it going?"

"Oh," she answered, "good, good."

I nodded at her, and she nodded back, and we stood there nodding at each other, neither one of us sure of what to say next. Finally, I looked over at the door she'd been trying to open. In clear, red-stenciled letters, it read, RESTRICTED ACCESS: APOGEE PERSONNEL ONLY.

I turned back to Ms. Kaufman, and before I could say anything, she started to laugh, flushing. "Holy smokes, I didn't even notice," she said, trying to sound surprised. "I got lost on my way back from the observation deck and I could've *sworn* this was my room!"

I looked at the door again. The words on it were pretty hard to miss. You'd have to *really* be in a fog to not see it was the kind of door you weren't supposed to open.

"I must be a little out of it from our trip," she went on.

"Sure, we all are," I assured her.

She nodded again, and I nodded again, and we stood there nodding some more, looking like those bobblehead dolls given away at baseball games.

"Well," she finally said, "I guess I'll go take a nap and clean up before dinner. That is, if I can find my room, ha-ha." Her laugh didn't sound very convincing.

"Ha-ha," I laughed back. "See you in a while."

She spun and walked away, turning a corner out of sight. I was left looking at the door.

RESTRICTED ACCESS: APOGEE PERSONNEL ONLY.

I wondered if maybe I shouldn't tell David Wong about what I'd just seen. Maybe Elaine was out snooping for ways she could slam Apogee in her article. But, then, there was always the chance that Ms. Kaufman was telling the truth. I decided I'd hold off on saying anything, but I'd definitely keep an eye on the travel reporter for the rest of our stay at Apogee.

Missing: One Dinner Guest

When I made it to the galley, I was the first one there—aside from various server robots, which moved all about the room, paying no attention to me at all. The table had been set, and while there were plates, there was no silverware. Makes sense, I thought. Anything we'd need silverware for would just float off the plate anyway.

At either end of the table were two large platters of tubes, each affixed to the plate by a strip of Velcro. The plate, in turn, was attached to the table with more Velcro. I picked one tube up. CHICKEN À LA KING, it read. I checked others. SHRIMP FRIED RICE. CHEESE ENCHILADAS. GARLIC TOAST. I couldn't help but smile. This was going to be a dinner unlike any other I'd ever experienced.

Sandy came in behind me and looked at the table. I heard her sigh.

"I was hoping there'd be at least a *little* solid food," she said.

"No such luck," I replied, gently floating a tube across the distance between us. "Here, have some crab puffs as an appetizer. You didn't happen to run into Elaine Kaufman on your way over here, did you?"

"No, but I did see Brendan." She opened the tube and squeezed some of the thick liquid inside into her mouth. Sandy paused thoughtfully, tasting it, then nodded in surprised approval. "Not bad! Anyway, I passed Brendan coming out of the gym. I told him I was going down to dinner, and invited him to come with me. But he just kept walking, saying he needed to be alone to think, and he'd see me later. Why are you wondering about Ms. Kaufman?"

Brendan Fogarty entered next and walked right past us to the table, where he sat down in a chair and started knocking his knuckles against the tabletop sullenly. "I'll tell you later," I said to Sandy, not wanting to discuss any of this in front of the other passengers.

"Where's your mom, Brendan?" Sandy asked.

"How should I know?" Brendan answered, not

looking up. "Probably buying a planet somewhere."

I decided to give friendship one more shot and sat down beside him. "Hey, man," I ventured. "What's bugging you? It seems like you've been bummed since before you got here."

"I'd rather be anywhere but here," he said.

"You don't think getting to go up in space is cool?"

"My *mother* thinks it's cool," Brendan responded sharply. "She just spends and spends and spends on whatever she wants. . . . She's never *asked* me if I want to go anywhere, she's just *assumed*, and dragged me along with her!"

Noticing the silence that followed his outburst, Brendan looked up, surprised to see Sandy and me looking at him, our expressions a mixture of concern and pity, I guess. He looked back down at the table and started knocking his knuckles again. "Not that it's any of your business," he added with a mutter.

The door whooshed open, and David Wong entered with Elaine Kaufman, who was furiously scribbling down into her little notebook every word he said. "No, I don't think Apogee has anything to fear from The Road Back or any other anti-space or anti-technology organization," he was saying.

"Progress is unstoppable. Space tourism is coming, and coming soon. Doing anything to sabotage this hotel is simply delaying the inevitable. Extremists like The Road Back focus on bigger, more serious targets."

"That's a pretty casual attitude, David," Ms. Kaufman said, raising her eyebrow. "All I asked was if there was going to be security aboard the hotel."

David sighed, exasperated. "Of course there will be, Ms. Kaufman," he assured her. "It isn't necessary for a special VIP event like this, but once we're up and running, we'll have a well-trained security team in place here at Apogee." He turned to us and smiled. "Hello, everyone—"

"Mr. Wong, one more question," Ms. Kaufman said, interrupting him.

"After dinner, all right, Ms. Kaufman? I'm just not good at defending what I do for a living on an empty stomach." He gave her a smile, but there wasn't much humor behind it, and he turned to us. "I assume that since he's not here, Dr. Gorinsky still isn't feeling well enough to join us."

Ms. Kaufman closed her notebook with an annoyed snap, smiled thinly, and walked to her chair. David looked around the room. "We're still missing someone," he said with a curious frown.

"My mom," Brendan huffed.

"Well, it's pretty rude to start without her," David said, and walked to the wall-mounted intercom system. "What's her room number? One-eleven?" He punched in the numbers and spoke into the microphone. "Ms. Fogarty? It's David Wong. We're meeting for dinner. Are you ready to join us? Ms. Fogarty?"

He waited for a few moments, but there was no answer. Frowning again, he punched another button. "Ms. Fogarty," he said, and I heard his voice echoing all around me. He was using the ship-wide intercom system. "Ms. Fogarty, please respond by pushing the white button on any intercom you happen to be near." Silence. "Ms. Fogarty?"

"Don't worry about her," Brendan said. "Sometimes she doesn't answer when we're in the same room!"

David pushed another button. "All stations, please report if you have seen one of our guests, Victoria Fogarty." A series of voices came through the intercom in response, all of them saying they hadn't seen the billionaire.

David frowned and adjusted his jacket. He pushed the button for the Command Center. "Patch a video feed for room one-eleven into the galley monitor, please."

Elaine Kaufman looked shocked. "You spy on your guests?" she huffed.

"Hardly," David assured her. "The cameras in the guest rooms—in all the rooms on the facility—are a safety measure insisted upon by the Transportation Safety Bureau. They can't be initiated or operated without the station commander's say-so. And I'm saying so."

"Video feed from room one-eleven," a voice announced from the intercom. We moved across the room to the large monitor on the opposite wall. Normally, it served as a screen for entertainment for those dining. Guests could survey the view from one of the station's external cameras, watch a documentary about the building of the hotel, or catch a sporting event on satellite television from Earth.

The screen flickered to life, calling up a view of Ms. Fogarty's room. It looked empty. "What's that?" Sandy asked, suddenly. She pointed to the side of the screen. We all leaned in, and to somebody walking in at that moment, it might have seemed funny except for what we were looking at: a woman's limp hand, floating just at the edge of the screen.

"Mom!" Brendan shouted.

"Pan camera slow left!" David yelled back over his shoulder toward the intercom, and the angle slowly swept to the side. Ms. Fogarty appeared to us in full, drifting in her room's microgravity, unconscious. She had one shoe on and one shoe off. I thought I saw a small smudge of some kind on her ankle, but I couldn't be sure.

"What happened to her?" Brendan demanded to know.

"I don't know," David replied grimly. "But I'm going to find out." He raced for the door, all of us behind him. The station manager yelled toward the intercom as he went by, "Get medical services to room one-eleven right away!"

A few moments later we stood outside the door to room one-eleven. One of the two medical technicians aboard the station was there waiting for us. Robots moved back and forth in the corridor behind us like afternoon traffic.

David pushed the doorbell on the panel next to the door. "Ms. Fogarty? It's David Wong. . . . Can you hear me?"

"Don't be an idiot," Brendan said, pushing past him. "My mother gave me the extra key to her room. Let's just go in!" He inserted his key card, and the door whooshed open.

It was empty.

Ms. Fogarty was nowhere to be seen. Her luggage was there, all the furniture was there, and there was no sign of a struggle. David moved to the intercom and called up the Command Center. "Wong to Command," he said. "Activate all station cameras. Is there any sign anywhere of Victoria Fogarty?" The answer came back quickly: Victoria Fogarty was nowhere to be found.

Elaine Kaufman raised her eyebrows and started writing in her notebook.

Despite the fact that he was a good six inches shorter than David, Brendan rushed up to the station manager and grabbed him by the front of his jacket. "Find my mom," he demanded. "You lost her, you find her!"

I wrestled Brendan away, which wasn't easy. He was a lot stronger than I expected. "Brendan, relax! Flipping out isn't going to help us find your mother!"

"She has to be on the station somewhere, right?"

Sandy pointed out. "It's not like she jumped off or anything." She turned to David. "A super-thorough search of the whole hotel should find her."

"That's what I was going to suggest," David said, his eyes squarely on Brendan. "I know you're upset, Brendan. I am too. But we can't go flying off the handle."

"You find my mom, or I will fly off the handle," Brendan promised in a low growl.

"She was unconscious when we saw her on the monitor," I said. "She could have woken up and wandered away."

David shook his head. "One of the cameras would have picked her up."

"Then someone must have moved her and hid her before the cameras were activated. Probably the same person who knocked her out."

Ms. Kaufman looked up from her notebook. "How do you know someone knocked her out?"

I looked over to David. "Can you call up the video we saw before in the galley?"

A moment later, we were looking at the earlier image of Ms. Fogarty, floating in the room in which we were now standing. "Can we push in on her ankle?" David manipulated some controls, and soon we were looking at the smudge I had noticed before on her ankle. "Right there," I said, pointing to it. "I think that's a burn mark. I think Ms. Fogarty was knocked out by an electrical shock. And," I said, pointing around the room, "it doesn't look like any of the lights or appliances shorted out. So that would suggest it was intentional."

"Who would have done it?" Brendan demanded to know.

"Well, it wasn't any of us," Ms. Kaufman said. "We were all in the galley together."

"No," Sandy pointed out, "the shock could have happened before we went to the galley. We don't know when that happened. All we know is that none of us moved her or hid her."

We all stood there, thinking over the questions that had appeared before us.

Then Brendan said what none of us had dared to say—the most frightening question of all: "We don't even know if my mom's still alive, wherever she is."

Marooned

We returned to the galley. With the station's skeleton crew, the search of the hotel would be a slow process. But David authorized the two crew members he could spare to scour the entire hotel from top to bottom for Victoria Fogarty.

While we waited, David used the galley monitor to call Earth and apprise Above and Beyond of the situation. Elaine Kaufman, meanwhile, gobbled everything in her condensed food tubes while writing long notes in her notebook. Then she finished everything in my tubes, and then in Sandy's.

"I can't help it," she said through a mouth full of food. "I was a crime reporter before I was a travel reporter, and I always get hungry when I'm on a really good story."

"Stop talking about my mother like she's just a story!" Brendan Fogarty demanded emotionally. He hadn't touched any of his food. "There could still be a simple explanation for all of this that we just haven't thought of! We don't even know if a crime's been committed!"

"Assuming a crime *has* been committed," David Wong said quietly, turning to the monitor on the wall. Giles Burton's solemn face stared back at him from the screen. "I think the best thing to do is have all of our guests return to Earth as soon as possible, for their own safety," David continued.

Giles nodded. "You're right. The authorities will meet you at Above and Beyond headquarters to question you and you'll remain there until Ms. Fogarty is located and this situation is resolved."

"We're being detained?!" Ms. Kaufman yelped incredulously.

"Ms. Kaufman," Giles said, "for the moment, unfortunately, you're all suspects in her disappearance. I expect we'll have found Ms. Fogarty long before your shuttle gets you home. . . . I'm just speaking in terms of worst-case scenario." He sighed heavily. "All right, everyone's coming home."

I could see the deep concern beneath Giles's features. Not only was he as worried about what might have happened to Ms. Fogarty as we were, he had to contend with the fact that a situation such as this aboard his hotel could be a fatal blow to any hope of making Apogee a working resort. But Giles—and David were trying hard to appear calm and poised. They were choosing their words very carefully, quite aware that there was a reporter in the room with them.

"And I'm sorry to have to do this," Giles continued, "but out of respect to Brendan's family, and in regard to any investigation, I'm afraid I'm going to have to restrict communication between all of you and Earth for the duration of your stay on Apogee, which I hope will be brief. The only communication between Apogee and home will be carried out by Apogee staff in the hotel's Command Center, under my orders."

"That's censorship!" shouted Ms. Kaufman, throwing down her pen with a clatter. It rebounded off the table and hung lazily before our eyes.

"I suppose it is," David said, nodding, "and you're welcome to lodge a complaint. When you get home."

The travel reporter sat back in her chair, clearly upset and disappointed. I think she'd lost her appetite.

"I don't expect much to come out of this," David continued, "but I should probably ask all of you where you were before you came to the galley."

Brendan threw up his hands. "You can't be asking *me* that question! Besides, there's not enough staff aboard to have seen us and back up whatever we say! "

David made calming gestures with his hands. "You're right, Brendan, we're not treating you as a suspect. As for backing up anyone's story, our housekeeping robots keep visual logs. And they're around enough that they almost certainly would have seen you at some point. So..." David turned to Sandy and me.

"We were in the rec room playing badminton," I told him.

"I won," Sandy interjected. I shot her a "not now" look.

"After the game, I came down here to the galley to see if I could get a snack before dinner."

"And I went back to my room," Sandy said. "I wanted to go to the observation deck, but my hammock was so comfy, I fell asleep instead!"

David scratched his head. "Did either of you see anything unusual or strange?"

"Actually, I did," I said. "But I don't know that it had anything to do with what happened to Ms. Fogarty. Coming down to the galley, I met up with Ms. Kaufman. She was trying to get in through a door that was restricted."

The travel reporter leaped out of her seat, her face turning bright red. "I told you—that was a mistake! I thought it was my room!"

"That's a pretty unusual mistake to make," David said, rubbing his eyes. "The doors are clearly marked, and the restricted doors use a different kind of card reader and even open horizontally, not vertically, like guest rooms or common areas."

He leaned across the table, looking her straight in the eye. "And those questions you were asking me before . . ."

"They were for my story," she bleated. "I'm a reporter!"

"Ms. Kaufman," David said coolly, "I've dealt with a lot of reporters, and you weren't so much asking questions as you were barely concealing accusations. Now I think you should tell us what's going on."

She looked around the room, as though someone, anyone, would help her out, but we all stayed silent.

Her shoulders sagged, and she sat back down. "Okay, I'll tell you."

"What did you do with my mom?!" Brendan shouted, pointing an accusing finger.

"I didn't do anything to her! I swear! What I was doing had nothing to do with that."

Giles leaned forward, closer to the monitor in his office. "Then what *did* it have to do with, Ms. Kaufman?"

She looked down at the table for a long moment, then back up at the hotel manager. "I *am* doing a story on Apogee for the magazine . . . but I'm also here working for someone else. Foger Utility Group."

"FUG?" I exclaimed in disbelief. "They're my dad's company's chief rival!"

"And they're total jerks!" Sandy added.

"They paid me to spy on the hotel," Ms. Kaufman went on. "They want to know all of Apogee's weaknesses so they can spread rumors that it's unsafe. But I haven't found anything," she added quickly, then continued, in a quieter, almost embarrassed voice, "except for, you know, what's happened with Ms. Fogarty. I may be a snoop, but I'm not violent, or a kidnapper . . . or a killer."

David nodded thoughtfully. "Okay," he said, rising

and moving to the intercom. Like the professional he was, he'd decided not to make an issue of Ms. Kaufman's activities. Finding out what happened to Ms. Fogarty was the priority. "I'll see about getting the shuttle ready to take you home."

He pushed a button on the intercom. "Flight Deck, this is David. How soon can the shuttle be ready for relaunch?"

Once again, there was no answer from the intercom. "I don't believe this," David muttered, and pushed the intercom button again, harder. "Flight Deck, this is David. Can you hear me?"

There was a tremendous blast of feedback, a shriek so loud, I had to clap my hands over my ears. "Flight Deck," David shouted into the intercom. "What's going on down there?!"

A voice burst through the static. We couldn't hear every word, but the panic and strain in the voice was evident. "Problem . . . here . . . Fire . . . out of control . . . fire . . . shuttle!"

On the monitor, Giles stood up from his desk. "David, get down there now!"

"On my way," David barked, and hurried out of the room. All of us followed, dodging housekeeping robots running this way and that as we tried to keep up with David's quick strides.

We raced to the corridor in the central core that led to the docking bay, to discover it was filled with thick, oily, black smoke. The floor was covered with a thin layer of chemical foam, which didn't affect traction since the floor was a sticky surface to begin with.

The technician who had spoken to us over the intercom leaned weakly against a wall, coughing spastically. David put a worried hand on his shoulder. "Can't see in there . . . ," the man said. "Too much smoke . . . foam . . ."

The air filters were clearly having trouble dealing with so much smoke at once, and the blackness of the hall started to grow.

"Get back, get back!" David yelled at us between coughs as he struggled to pull himself forward to the dock by feel. Sandy and Brendan and Elaine obeyed, but I kept moving forward. If someone was hurt, maybe I could help. I lifted my shirt front over my mouth. The smoke stung my eyes, making them water.

I could just barely see David up ahead of me, coughing loudly as he stepped through the waist-deep foam into the docking chamber. I followed him in and could hear the ceiling-mounted foam dispensers' constant hiss as they tried to smother the flames, which I still couldn't see.

David struggled forward another step, and then a blast of foam caught him square on the head, its force driving him to his knees—and under the surface of the foam layer!

"David!" I shouted, but I could hear no human voice over the alarm Klaxons and the hiss of the extinguishers. David was drowning!

I stumbled farther into the room, sweeping my hands below the foam line, hoping to come into contact with something—or someone—solid. Foam jets lanced down all around me. I did my best to avoid them—and stay on my feet. Pulling myself through the foam felt like swimming in dense shaving cream.

At last, my hands closed around something tubular. An arm? I yanked it to the surface only to find I was holding some manner of thick cable. I dropped it and returned to my sweeping. David couldn't possibly have much time left!

Luckily, a few steps later my knee hit something solid that didn't feel like metal. Reaching down, I pulled David up by the shoulders. He was unconscious. I reached my arm under his and across his chest. Much like rescuing a drowning surfer, I "swam" him back out of the room, taking care to keep his head above the level of the foam.

A few moments later we were back out in the corridor, and clear of the foam and smoke. I laid David down, and he immediately started coughing . . . a good sign. I was coughing myself and I could barely stand up. Sandy rushed over to support me while Elaine helped David regain consciousness. "What was on fire?" Sandy asked. "Did you see?" I could only shake my head.

After a time, the alarms stopped and a horde of the small robots rushed into the corridor with hoses attached, sucking up all the leftover foam. The hall was clear now, but still smoky. David staggered to his feet. "Take it easy," Elaine said to him. "Are you sure you're okay?"

"I'm fine," David replied, still coughing slightly. "Is the station okay? That's the real question." I had to admire his devotion to Apogee. David turned to me. "That was a pretty stupid thing you did, following me in there."

"I know," I admitted.

"Thanks," he said seriously.

"You're welcome."

We moved down the corridor to the docking chamber. Nothing in here seemed burned. David leaned in through the shuttle door for a peek inside. "Unbelievable," David moaned as we all craned our necks to look past him at the shuttle's cockpit.

The main pilot console was burned black, scorched. The smell of roasted wiring and metal was thick. Not a single light shone anywhere in the cockpit.

"That's the navigation computer, as well as the manual backups," said David. "Someone knew exactly what they were busting up."

"They didn't even try to be sneaky about it," I added, perplexed.

"Does this have anything to do with my mother?" Brendan wanted to know, poking in his head.

"We can't know, Brendan. Let's get on the horn to Earth," David said to the tech. "See how fast they can get another shuttle up here."

"Yeah," Elaine replied from outside, "there's a problem with that, too." We exited the shuttle, passed through the air lock, and walked back into the operations center of the Flight Deck, where the docking controls were.

The tech pointed to one of the many monitors in the room. This one was a large map of South America. There was an angry red splotch over Brazil, surrounded by yellow smears and green dots. "If these weather satellites are right, Brazil's socked in by a major storm." David pressed a button, and the picture changed to real-time video of Rio's streets. Rain fell in sheets from a solid gray sky, and wind whipped the trees back and forth. "Everything's shut down, down there, and the storm has even caused minor damage to Above and Beyond's launch facilities," David said, looking at a digital readout below the monitor. "Nothing's going in or out of there anytime soon."

"But my mother!" Brendan blurted.

"We'll keep looking, Brendan, but we'll have to do it with you here," David replied, rubbing his eyes again. He still sounded calm and poised, but his face was smudged by smoke and he looked very, very tired. I can't say I blamed him.

He sighed heavily. "This just gets better and better."

10

Putting It Together

Later that night, I lay in my hammock, staring at the ceiling (I think it was the ceiling . . .), trying to put together the events of the day in my mind. The search for Victoria Fogarty was continuing, still without success so far. I could still taste smoke in my throat and could feel the raspiness in my lungs. But I'd cleaned up with some of the large, moist towelettes and was feeling much better, all in all.

After going over everything for the fiftieth time, I realized I was actually pretty comfortable. Lying down or resting in microgravity really wasn't too bad—it felt a lot like being on a raft in the middle of a pool, only without the sensation of something holding you up.

These thoughts actually irked me a little bit

because they made me remember how much I would have been enjoying myself if it hadn't been for the disappearance of Ms. Fogarty. Then I got mad at myself for thinking so selfishly. *Imagine what Brendan's going through*, I thought. Hopefully, he was right. Maybe there was a simple explanation for her disappearance. Maybe she woke from her electrical jolt disoriented and wandered somewhere the station's cameras couldn't see her—a supply closet, maybe. It wasn't likely, but it was possible. If so, the search team would find her, sooner or later.

The intercom in the wall next to my bed beeped. I answered it. "Hello?"

"Tom? Did I wake you up?" It was Sandy. She didn't sound sleepy at all.

"No," I assured her. "Are you all right? Do you want to come over?"

"I'm fine. I was just wondering . . . could you actually come over *here*?"

I started unwrapping myself from the sleeping bag. "Sure," I told her. "Be right there."

Sandy was only one module over from me, so it wasn't exactly a long walk. I just pulled on my slippers and stepped out into the hall and through the lock that connected the two inflatable segments. I was alone, of course, but now the silence was eerie, as though we were on a ghost ship. *There's a saboteur on Apogee*, I reminded myself. *We're all in danger.*

There were even fewer of the small "Jeeves" robots racing around than usual. "Night" was kind of an arbitrary concept on a space hotel—it was always dark outside. But at certain prescribed hours, computers tinted all the windows to minimize the amount of light coming through the viewports to simulate nighttime. I took the few steps to Sandy's door and rang her intercom. "Tom?" I heard her ask tentatively.

"Of course," I said. "Who else?"

The door rose up with its customary whoosh and I walked inside. Every light in the room was on. Sandy was halfway up one of the walls, swaddled tightly in her bunk. Her eyes were wide, and she quickly pushed the button to close the door again. "What's up?" I asked. She didn't answer.

I stepped out of my slippers and jumped lightly, letting the lack of gravity allow me to float upward until I stopped myself by grabbing hold of one of the hammock support pegs. I was now able to look Sandy in the eye. "Sandy? What's going on?"

"It's-it's just weird," she said haltingly. "I mean, how am I supposed to sleep when there's a saboteur out there?"

"How do you know I'm not the saboteur?" I asked gravely.

She thumped me on the arm, hard. "That's not funny! I'm serious! If someone hurt Ms. Fogarty, we could be next!"

"I doubt it," I assured her. "If a saboteur's trying to make the hotel look bad, he wouldn't need to attack more than one high-profile guest. And if he were trying to take over the station, he wouldn't have attacked Ms. Fogarty at all, but David or one of his crew."

"He or *she*," Sandy interjected. "We don't know the saboteur is a man, necessarily."

"Okay, but do you see what I'm saying?"

"I guess." Sandy sighed. "But none of this is making me feel any better," she said. I didn't have an answer for her. I wasn't feeling any better either.

Abruptly, the door whooshed open again, and both Sandy and I jumped a little. She hadn't hit the button on her wall panel, and I wasn't anywhere near it—who else could be coming in?

We got our answer as a little housekeeping robot whirred in, carrying a small stack of plastic-wrapped, moist towelettes for Sandy's bathroom. She burrowed further into her bunk. "Okay, that's just creepy," she said. "Just knowing that I could be sleeping and one of those things could come into my room and I'd never know it. . . ."

She trailed off as I watched the robot roll to the sink to deposit its payload of towels. Before it could, though, it stopped, and I could hear clicking sounds coming from inside it. The small antenna jutting from its top glowed blue as it received signals from a central command. Its message received, the little robot deposited the towels and headed back out the door, which closed behind it.

Sandy shuddered again. "Brrr . . . I wish I knew how to lock those things out!"

Her voice seemed to be coming from farther and farther away. I stared without seeing at the towels stacked on the sink. My brain was working, possibilities turning over and over, pieces clicking into place. When I get going like that, the entire world disappears around me. It's a strange, amazing feeling, like you're traveling to an entirely other place that no one else can find but you.

"Tom? Tom?" Sandy asked more and more urgently, her voice becoming louder and louder. She snapped her fingers in front of my face. I turned and smiled at her. "What happened? Where did you go?"

"We have to find David, right away," I said excitedly.

"Why? What's the matter?"

"Nothing," I said, turning myself over to point at the floor. I pushed off the support post and drifted down to the ground and my slippers. "I just figured out what happened to Ms. Fogarty!"

11

Kidnapping by Remote Control

"I've totally got the *how* figured out, I'm just not sure of the *why* . . . or the *who* that was behind it. . . ."

David Wong yawned and tucked his shirt in as we walked down the quiet corridor. His eyes were bloodshot, and there were dark crescents under his eyes. He hadn't even tried to sleep; he was waiting by the intercom for any word that might come in from the search party when Sandy and I came calling with my urgent discovery. I felt bad bothering him, but knew he wanted to find Ms. Fogarty as bad as anyone. "Then let's start with the *how*," he said.

We arrived at a door marked MECHANICAL DIS-PATCH, and David used his key card to get us inside. The room was filled with robots—the small ones we

had seen so many of, and the taller ones that carried larger quantities of supplies in their chest cavities. Some were on workbenches, awaiting repair, while most of the rest were lined up before various doors, ready to be called into action.

I walked over to one of the taller robots standing quietly on the floor, and reached up to touch its signal antenna. "All of these are wired into the main power grid of the hotel, right?"

"Yeah," David said, a touch of worry in his voice. "Hey, don't touch the—"

My finger brushed the top of the antenna, and an electrical jolt went through me, knocking me flat on my butt. It wasn't a powerful burst, but it was enough to surprise me and set my heart racing. "That's a pretty good zap!" I exclaimed.

"But not enough to shock Ms. Fogarty into unconsciousness," Sandy said, frowning.

"All of our robots are programmed to carry a maximum load of energy when on duty," David pointed out. "Accidental contact with one of our housekeepers shouldn't knock out *anyone*."

I raised a finger. "Not when they're operating *normally*," I said. "The robots receive their signals and their communications through these antennae, right?"

David scratched his head, messing up his hair even further. "Sure. Radio waves."

"Right! And theoretically, someone with a transmitter could tap into that frequency and deliver his or her own orders to any particular robot!"

Sandy's eyes lit up. "Someone reprogrammed one of these bigger robots to carry more electricity than usual, sent it to Ms. Fogarty's room, and had it knock her out!"

I nodded. "And then, I'm guessing, they had the robot put Ms. Fogarty in its storage compartment and take her to some hiding place. I just don't know where."

Sandy's face flushed with excitement as she followed my line of thinking. "I bet a robot ruined the shuttle's computer too! Maybe even the same robot, to cut down on the chances of the criminal being discovered!"

I held my hand up for a high five, and Sandy smacked it.

David walked around the little robot in a tight circle, as though seeing it in a new way. "Okay, it's *possible*. But who would do it?"

"Well," I confessed, "that's the *why*, and the part I'm not sure about. I guess anyone on your staff with a knowledge of how the robots work could have done it."

David shook his head, unsure. "That's a lot of people, and most of them have worked for Above and Beyond for a long time. Everyone goes through a pretty strict screening before they join the company or the project." He sighed. "Now we have to think—where could Ms. Fogarty be that we haven't already looked? The robot didn't bring her back here, obviously."

There was a sudden chorus of beeps in the room, as all of the robots seemed to hear the same message at the same time. It startled all of us, and Sandy even grabbed on to my sleeve, worried that maybe the robots had gone haywire again. They started to jabber to one another, trading information and statements until they seemed to come to a decision, and four of the smaller robots started right toward us!

We backed up a few steps as the "housekeepers" advanced, their antennae flashing. Just before they got to us, however, they split into pairs, two exiting a door to our left, two going out a door to our right.

Even though they were gone, I could tell we all were still nervous, each thinking the same thought: *Had a saboteur suddenly taken over those four robots?*

David, apparently, knew we were all thinking in sync too. "Let's not get too worried just yet," he said, moving to the intercom. "Wong to all Apogee personnel," he said into it. "Did someone just order a late-night snack?"

"Ryan here, Dave," a voice came back. "We just sent down for some sandwiches. Can we get you one?"

"No thanks, I was just checking. Housekeepers are on their way to the galley to get your grub. Enjoy your bite." He snapped the intercom off and turned back to us, sighing in relief. "Okay, no problem there. Guess you've got *me* spooked, now."

We all laughed a little, the tension easing slightly.

"I suppose the first thing we should do is shut down all the robot personnel for the time being. That'll make for a tired human crew, as we'll all be doing jobs the robots normally would, but better safe than sorry," he said.

"Would that even work?" Sandy wanted to know, her voice tinged with worry. "I mean, if someone has a remote control that can reprogram the robots, they could probably also turn the robots on and off, right?"

David's face scrunched up as though he smelled something unpleasant, then he relaxed into a resigned smile. "That's a very good point."

I drummed my fingers on a workbench, still stuck on wondering who might have ordered a robot to hurt Ms. Fogarty. My thoughts turned immediately to Elaine Kaufman. The travel writer had a motive, namely making Apogee look bad both for her article, and for Foger. But I couldn't picture her having the technological knowledge necessary to pull off "hijacking" a housekeeping robot. Ms. Kaufman couldn't figure out a way past the key card system into that restricted corridor.

And then there was Dr. Gorinsky, but there wasn't anything unusual about him, except he'd been in sick bay most of the day, and . . .

And . . .

"Hey," I blurted to Sandy as soon as I had the thought. "Do you remember how Dr. Gorinsky kept trying to avoid Ms. Fogarty, and how she swore she'd met him before?"

Sandy nodded. "Yeah, she brought it up twice, and both times he acted like he couldn't change the subject fast enough!"

David looked at us as if we'd lost our minds. "The man's got a résumé as long as your arm. . . . He's one of the most respected scientists in the world! Do you really think he's hiding something?"

"I don't know," I said, already heading for the door and pointing myself toward sick bay. "But I think it's worth asking him a few questions!"

12

The Good Doctor

The three of us raced to the infirmary. All of the beds were unoccupied, and the medical tech on duty was making notes on a chart.

"Dr. Gorinsky," David said breathlessly. "Is he here?"

The med tech looked up and blinked, confused. "Dr. Gorinsky? He checked out of here hours ago, saying he was feeling much better. I even gave him some decongestant for his sinuses. I figured he had gone back to his room. Is something up, David?"

David ignored him and rushed to an intercom. "Dr. Gorinsky, this is David Wong. Please respond." There was no answer. "Dr. Gorinsky?" Silence. David tried the ship-wide intercom, but got the same result.

"Should we split up and look for him?" I asked.

"No," David replied. "I think the two of you should go back to your rooms and secure the doors until we can locate Dr. Gorinsky. I'm locking down this hotel as of right now. Nobody moves through our corridors except my personnel. Program your doors with the privacy code, zero-zero-zero-zero-one. That should keep out the housekeeping robots."

"But—" I interjected.

"No buts," he said firmly, albeit with a smile. "I know you're the kids of our major investors, but I'm hotel manager and I'm pulling rank. Let me and my staff handle this. I'm heading up to the Command Center. It's not far from here. You two go on, now."

He turned and strode away from us, back out into the quiet hall and out of the module. Sandy and I followed him out and stood just outside the door. We stood there quietly for a moment, then Sandy said, "We're not really going to let him send us to our room, are we? I mean, that's not the kind of thing we usually let happen to us when stuff like this is going on."

I thought about it. Sandy was right. Usually, we were only too eager to jump right in and help with any situation. This time, though, there was a chance we could cause more damage than good. "I think we'd better do what David says," I told Sandy. "Neither one of us has been in space before, David knows the ins and outs of this a whole lot better than we do, and it may just be smarter to lie low." Sandy gave me a sour look. "At least for now," I added.

Sandy sighed and nodded reluctantly. Then she scrunched up her face. "I just had a scary thought," she said. "What if Dr. Gorinsky isn't hiding out somewhere? What if the same thing happened to him that happened to Ms. Fogarty?"

"I guess we'll find out soon enough. Just like Ms. Fogarty, there aren't too many places he can be on the station, and he couldn't leave if he wanted to," I pointed out.

"You're right." She sighed as we started walking to our respective modules. We walked in silence for a while, but then, when we got to the junction lock where we had to split to go our separate ways, we ran into Brendan Fogarty. Or, rather, he ran into us. His face was bright red, and he looked angrier than anyone I think I've ever seen.

"Where's David Wong? Have you seen him?

What's he doing about my mother? He better not be sleeping!"

On cue, David's voice came over the ship-wide intercom. His face appeared beside it on a video screen. "Attention all personnel and guests. This is hotel manager David Wong. I'm instituting a full lockdown of Apogee, effective immediately. All guests, please return to your rooms, and all off-duty personnel, please return to your quarters until further notice. Thank you for your cooperation."

Brendan's expression changed from anger to hopefulness. "Do you think he has a lead on what happened to my mother? Is that what this is all about?"

"I'm sure you'll be the first person to know, Brendan," I assured him. "But for now, we'd better do as David says and get back to our rooms."

He nodded anxiously and went back the way he came. Sandy and I looked at each other. "If you need me and you don't want anyone else to hear it, call me on the Swift Speak," I told her, patting the tiny transceiver in my pocket, where it sat next to Joao's medallion. I sure had my suspicions about that medallion's ability to make this trip safe! "Everything's going to be fine."

"I hope you're right," she said, and walked quickly away to her room. I made sure I saw her step inside, then headed for my own quarters.

Once I was inside, I set the door lock as David had instructed. Now there wasn't much to do but sit around and wait. To pass the time for a while, I took off my slippers and practiced moving around in microgravity. It was fun, but even something as cool as floating weightless can get old, especially when you have a lot of things on your mind. Where was Victoria Fogarty? Where was Dr. Gorinsky? What would all of this mean for Apogee . . . and Swift Enterprises? Elaine Kaufman was bound to write a bad review now—if she really was a journalist, like she claimed. Would she ruin Above and Beyond? Would everything Giles Burton had worked for go down the drain?

Returning to the ground, I opened my luggage and rooted around until I found my jetpack. I'd almost forgotten I'd even packed it. Looking at it made me a little sad. I'd wanted to try it out on some space walks, but now it didn't look like that was going to happen at all. How could this trip have gone so wrong?

I looked out my viewport. I had an amazing view of Earth, and specifically Europe, though it was in shadow because that side of the planet was in the middle of the night. But I saw brilliant small clusters of light spread across the land masses, and it took me a minute to realize what I was looking at: They were major cities. I recognized Paris, and London, and Madrid.

Finally, bored of counting cities and anxious, I switched on my intercom. "Tom Swift to Command Center," I said. "David, is there any news? Is there any word from the search party?"

"David can't come to the intercom," a voice replied.

I frowned. "Is he there? Who is this?"

"This is the person who will show the world the folly of technological advancement, that the further we go scientifically, the further we get from the natural world that created us!"

Uh-oh.

"Okay," I said, "but that's kind of a lot to call you when we're having a conversation. Do you maybe have a *name*?"

"Activate your video," the voice said.

Nervously I thumbed the button, and the video screen next to the speaker flickered to life. It showed David Wong, frightened and angry, tied up to a chair with nylon cord! "David!" I exclaimed.

"No, that's *his* name," the voice said mockingly.

The camera changed angle, panning to show Ms. Fogarty, still unconscious but obviously breathing, also tied to a chair. I felt a surge of relief despite the tension of the situation; at least she was still alive. "And I take it you know *her* name," the voice said.

The camera continued to pan, finally revealing the voice's owner. He was a thin, balding man, who used to have an absentminded look in his eyes. But now his eyes were slitted and angry, alight with triumph. "You know me as 'Peter Gorinsky,' but my real name is Lars Haas . . . and I claim this technological abomination of a hotel you call Apogee in the name of The Road Back!"

Double uh-oh.

13

Hostages

I watched on video as Haas touched his cheek and chin, smiling, pleased. "The plastic surgeons, did a nice job, didn't they? I look just like Peter Gorinsky!"

He looked around the Command Center, then down at David, who gritted his teeth helplessly. "This is a lovely Command Center you have here. Why, you can indeed control everything on Apogee from here. Such as . . ." Haas leaned forward and pushed a button, almost experimentally.

There was a thudding noise from inside the lock mechanism for the door to my room. I rushed to it, but it wouldn't open. I pulled out my Swift Speak and fit it into my ear. "Sandy, are you all right?"

"I'm fine," my sister answered, "but my door won't open!"

"Security override on all door mechanisms," I heard Haas say. "Nice feature. Sometimes, technology *does* have its uses. Now, even though I know you're all safely tucked away in your rooms, in case you have any ideas whatsoever of trying to escape before my mission is complete, I thought I'd show you why it's not a good idea."

He reached for another button. David leaned forward in his chair, straining, trying to reach out to stop him, but was unable to free his arms. "No! Don't—!"

Haas pressed the button, and there was a hollow booming noise, like someone had fired a cannon, and then the entire hotel shook. Had Haas set off some kind of explosive aboard Apogee?

I scrambled to my viewport and craned my neck around as far as it would go in all directions, trying to see if there was any damage to the hotel. I didn't see any tears in the hull, or any dislodged or wrecked antennae . . . but I did see one of the hotel's inflatable modules drift by—Haas had released it, setting it free from its docking port to float out of control in the emptiness of space! Cold fear wrapped its hands around my heart. Was Brendan Fogarty in there? Or Elaine Kaufman? Or somebody from David's crew?

"Now, don't anybody get worried," I heard Haas say. "There weren't any guests or hotel personnel in that module. That was just a demonstration. Mess with me, and you're going on a very long trip, one way."

"What is it you want, Haas?" I asked.

"Oh, I've got everything I want," he answered. "All I ever wanted was to get into this Command Center. And I would have done it sooner if it hadn't been for that Fogarty woman. . . ."

"You hurt my mom!" I heard Brendan shout over the intercom, and I realized that Haas had patched all of our rooms in together so he could talk to all of us at once.

"Yes, sorry about that." He didn't sound very apologetic. "I wasn't expecting to run into someone who knew Gorinsky from so long ago. I couldn't let her see through my disguise, so I rigged up a robot to eliminate her as a concern. Then I used that same robot to disable your shuttle so you'd be here as my hostages, which is what I wanted all along. I didn't like having to use so much technology to sabotage other technology, but again, it does have its uses at times, and in this case, it was necessary."

"You were right, Tom," Sandy said into my ear, using the Swift Speak. "The same robot committed both crimes." I nodded.

Elaine Kaufman's voice crackled through the speaker. "So, you're in the Command Center now, Haas. . . . Why do you need us?"

Haas laughed. "I would think it's pretty obvious, Ms. Kaufman. . . . I need you for leverage." He turned to the communications console and pressed buttons. "Apogee to Above and Beyond Ground Control."

"Ground Control," I heard Giles Burton say. "Go ahead, Apogee. Has there been any progress into the investigation of Ms. Fogarty's disappearance? I have the press down here asking how the mission is going, and it's getting hard to stall them."

"Tell them they have a bigger story to think about, Ground Control. My name is Lars Haas, I represent The Road Back, and control of this hotel is in my hands. You see, your former station manager, here, is my prisoner. And so is Victoria Fogarty."

"David!" Giles gasped. "Haas, you madman! Give me back my hotel, or I'll—"

"Or you'll what?" Haas asked in a mocking voice.

"Here's what you'll do: You will honor my demands, or there will be consequences." He waited, smiling. There was nothing any of us could do.

There was a long pause, then: "Go ahead, Apogee. State your demands."

Haas nodded his head. "Excellent. Someone clearly advised you to play along, to buy time until I could be taken down. Well, that's not going to happen, so you might as well take my demands seriously." I could imagine Giles's face hearing this, turning redder than ever before. Nobody likes to feel helpless.

Haas looked triumphantly at all of us through the monitor. "My demands are very simple, Ground Control: I want the release of every single incarcerated Road Back operative from their prisons around the world—"

"That's impossible!" Giles spluttered. "Be reasonable, Haas, give us something to work with—!"

". . . or," Haas continued, as though he hadn't even heard the objection, "if my demands are not met in a timely manner, I will release the rooms of this hotel's guests into space, never to be recovered. And I don't think you want that. After all, there are some high-profile guests aboard, like a prominent journalist, a decorated astronaut, the fourth—excuse me, third—richest woman on Earth and her son, and the son and daughter of the man who helped build this pimple on the face of human achievement!"

"This is insane," Giles's voice cried from Earth. He sounded very far away. "How do you expect us to—"

"I expect a report of positive progress in one hour," Haas said curtly. Hearing this, I quickly set the stopwatch function on my watch for one hour. "If I don't like what I hear, it's off into the 'wild black yonder' for one of these tourists. Apogee out."

He clicked off the communication to Earth and looked at us over the monitor proudly. "Swift brats, you can relax."

"You mean you're not going to kill us?" Sandy asked.

"Oh no, I will for sure. But not until last. As my biggest bargaining chips, it's in my best interests to hold on to you as long as I can. Brendan, you'll be the first to go. As long as I have your mother, you're of no use to me whatsoever."

"You jerk!" Brendan shouted, his voice breaking and on the edge of tears. "I hate you!"

"Ooh, that really hurts," Haas said mockingly. "Okay, everyone. Behave yourselves. Talk to you in an hour." The video screen went blank, and the intercom turned off. I checked to see if there was any way I could use the intercom to contact Earth, but of course I couldn't. Haas had blocked all transmissions except for those going from the Command Center to the rooms and back. We couldn't even talk to one another.

But I could talk to Sandy. There was no way for Haas to jam the Swift Speak. "Sandy, are you there?"

"I'm here, Tom," she answered back. "What are we going to do?"

"I'm working on that," I told her, looking around my room. There wasn't much to look at. Just the hanging hammock, the few pieces of furniture, the emergency air lock (which was only there in case a guest was trapped in the room and the only opportunity for rescue came from a tricky shuttle-to-inflatable docking . . . so *that* was of no use to me), and my luggage.

My luggage.

"Sandy, I've got a plan," I said quickly, pulling my space suit from my luggage. "But I'm going to need your help. Is there any way you can cause some kind of distraction when I give you the go-ahead over the Swift Speak?"

"I don't know how," she said.

"Well, I need you to think of something," I said urgently, "because my whole plan depends on it."

"What do you have in mind?" Sandy asked. She sounded evenly balanced between excited and worried.

"I don't have time to tell you . . . I don't know how long this next part will take."

"Hopefully less than an hour," she said dryly.

I had to laugh a little bit. It felt good to have the tension ease even slightly. "Just be ready when I say so," I told her, "and stay close to your Swift Speak."

I walked back to the intercom, making sure that there was no way Haas could see the open suitcase behind me, and the space suit inside. "Tom Swift to Haas."

Haas's smug face appeared on my monitor. "I hope you're not calling to beg, because that would be so embarrassing. . . ."

"You're not going to get away with this, you know. . . ."

Haas snorted. "What? You think your father won't

do everything in his power to make sure his little babies get home safe? I'll get away with this. I'll get away with anything I like. And I'll be a hero to The Road Back. It'll be the organization's greatest triumph, and my name will be remembered forever!"

"*If* you don't mess it up," I pointed out.

"Tom, stop—!" David Wong said urgently from behind Haas.

"What are you talking about?" he asked in disbelief. "I've already won! I've turned technology against its makers! How symbolic is that? *And* I'm going to free more of The Road Back's brightest minds, who will follow in my footsteps! Soon, Earth will be where *we* want it to be, where it always *should* have stayed!"

"Yeah, brilliant plan," I said with a smirk. "You're a tech-hating know-nothing in control of one of the most advanced satellites ever created! How ever much you learned before tricking your way onboard, there's no way you understand all of how Apogee works! You'll foul this up, trust me!"

Haas's face reddened, and he jabbed a finger at the monitor. "Don't try to mess with my head, twerp! It won't work! I'll just cut you loose, and then we'll see how you like it, starving out there in outer space! Or maybe your air will run out, and you'll suffocate! Or the heaters will fail, and you'll freeze! Does that sound good to you? Should I do that? Huh?"

"Tom, for pete's sake, cut it out," David urged.

"Oh yeah, that'd be a smart move," I replied, ignoring David and pushing Haas further. "What did you call my sister and me? Your 'biggest bargaining chips'? And you'd shoot me into space for giving you a hard time? Yeah, you're a regular genius!"

"Listen—" I could almost feel his anger rising, right through the intercom.

"No, *you* listen," I shouted. "You as much as *told* me I was untouchable! I'm in this to the very end! You'll *lose*, Haas! And I'm going to be here to watch you go down!"

Haas pressed his lips together very tightly, and his whole head shook as he turned an even deeper shade of red. He looked like he was about to explode all over David and the Command Center. "You think so, do you? You think your father wouldn't work just as hard to save one of you as he would both? Do you think I really need you *and* your sister?" he asked quietly. Then he reached for more buttons on the console.

"W-wait," I said, suddenly. "What are you doing?"

"Hello again, Apogee guests and staff, this is your new host, Lars Haas," he said into the intercom system, patching it in to all of the rooms. "It appears one of you isn't taking my promises seriously."

I waved my arms frantically, trying to get Haas's attention. "Haas, *stop!*"

But Haas continued. Either he didn't notice, or he did notice and just didn't want to acknowledge me. "And if one of you isn't taking me seriously, then that means the good folks on Earth might not either, so I think it's best to do something a little drastic. So, watch this, and rest assured that if any of you give me any trouble, I'll do exactly the same thing to you."

He moved to the panel that controlled the docking and undocking of the inflatable modules that housed the guest rooms. His finger hovered over a button.

"Haas, I'm sorry!" I screamed. "It was a joke! I was kidding! I'll stop! I'll—I'll be good!"

He looked up into the monitor and smiled coldly. "Good-bye, Tom."

He pressed the button, and there was another hollow booming sound, and then my monitor went dead. The entire room started to angle on its side, tilting gently over.

I pulled myself quickly over to the viewport and looked out. Apogee was slowly growing smaller, pulling away from my eyes. There was a big, empty space between two inflatable modules, where mine had been once before. Soon, Apogee would be just a dot among the millions of other stars in the black landscape. So would the moon. So would Earth. Haas had cut me loose.

I was adrift in outer space.

14

Extra-Vehicular Activity

"TOOOOOOOOMMM!!!"

Sandy's shriek was so loud in my Swift Speak earpiece that I actually felt my eardrum vibrate. "I'm here, Sandy," I said, wincing. "You don't have to yell!" I moved back to my suitcase, picked up my space suit, and started climbing into it.

"Are you okay?" she asked breathlessly. "How can we get you back? What are you going to do?"

"Sandy, relax," I urged her. "I needed him to detach my module from Apogee. Now he thinks I'm gone and won't be a problem for him anymore! He won't be watching me! This was all part of my plan."

Just from the sound of her voice, I could perfectly picture the confused look on her face. "It was? When you started to panic, I—"

"You were amazed at my acting talents, just like Haas!"

I heard her laugh with tired relief. "Tom Swift, if you ever do anything like that again, I'll . . . I'll . . . !"

Now it was my turn to laugh, as I zipped up my suit. "Now, have you found something you can use to start a distraction?"

"No, I—wait . . . yes, I think I've got it!"

"Cool. Be ready," I told her firmly. "When I say so, you do whatever it is."

I could hear the worry and uncertainty in her voice. "Tom, what are you going to do?"

Explaining everything in detail would take too long. . . . My module was drifting farther and farther away from Apogee with every second. "Sandy, I've got to stop communication for a little while. I need to concentrate. Just wait for my signal."

"But—"

I hated to cut her off, but she'd understand the big picture soon enough. I pulled the helmet over my head and sealed it, then started the space suit's oxygen supply. There was enough for three hours, but hopefully I wouldn't need nearly that much.

Hearing only the sound of my own breathing,

loud and ominous in my ears, I pulled the small jet-pack from my suitcase next. I had solved many of the design and functionality issues in putting it together, but not all of them. The amount of compressed air it stored as fuel was still relatively small. And I had used some of it blasting that protester off our limo back in Brazil, outside Above and Beyond's gates. The jetpack would allow me to maneuver in space . . . but not for very long. If there wasn't enough air to operate the thrusters and get me back to Apogee—or if I miscalculated and flew past Apogee without enough to turn me around and shoot me the other way—I'd wind up as adrift in space as if I'd stayed in my module.

So I was only going to get one chance. I slung the jetpack over my shoulders, like a backpack, and folded down the handles, with their buttons and joysticks that controlled the amount of thrust I used and its direction. I walked to the emergency air-lock exit, removed the plastic shield around the red handle, and took several deep breaths. This was it. Apogee and the lives of everyone aboard, including my sister's—not to mention my own—were in my hands. I pulled the handle.

As the red siren light started to spin, the heavy air-lock door slid up. Without a ship connected to the air lock on the other side, anything that wasn't nailed down in my room was immediately sucked from the module and out into the vacuum of space. My open suitcase went flying, all my clothes tumbling out into the darkness beyond the door. I thought how strange it would be for an alien ship, maybe millions of years from now, to stumble across a pair of my underwear floating in its path.

But I only had a moment to contemplate it because I was the next thing sucked out into the void! I had planned on using my thrusters to power myself out of the module and toward Apogee, but I'd forgotten that I wasn't nailed down either, and I was just as subject to the rapid decompression of the module as anything else.

I was so startled that I flailed my arms and legs a bit, trying to stay inside the module but, of course, I failed. My heart started to race, and the sound of my breathing magnified to an almost unbearable level. In flailing, though, I accidentally touched one of my thruster buttons. Now I had a real problem. Because I was off balance when I shot out into the vacuum, hitting the thruster, which released just a tiny puff of compressed air, was enough to send me turning head over heels. It was hard to focus my eyes on anything, but as I spun wildly, I could see both the module and the space hotel growing smaller and smaller. I was flying *away* from where I wanted to go! And because there was nothing to stop or slow my trajectory, if I didn't do something very quickly with my thrusters, I'd be flying a long way for a long time!

Luckily, when I have a problem to focus on, I'm able to put all other things aside—like fear. My breathing became more regular. But still, figuring out exactly when to fire my thrusters, to stop my headlong rotation without sending me tumbling back the other way, or in some other direction that wouldn't bring me any closer to where I wanted to be, wasn't easy. For one thing, I was getting dizzy. For another, I had to calculate how much thrust I needed to leave me pointed precisely in the direction of Apogee. I did my best to time my spin by the appearance of the two objects nearest me—Apogee and the module— but really, it came down to a guess, at the end. I hit the thrusters for a count of two and hoped for the best.

There was no sound, of course, as the thrusters released their compressed air, but I felt the effect immediately. My rotation and forward motion slowed, slowed some more, then stopped completely. I'd done it! I'd even come to rest facing Apogee! The only glitch was that I was upside down.

That may not sound like a glitch, but trust me. There was no way to right myself, whether on my own or with the thrusters, without sending me spinning all over again or pushing me way off course. If I was going to get back to Apogee, I was going to have to do it upside down.

A few years ago, my family went to Maui for a "vacation." I say "vacation" lightly because the Swift family doesn't really take vacations. Every place we visit is an opportunity to do some kind of scientific research, and going to Hawaii was no different: My dad wanted to check out some of the long-range radio telescopes housed on the island.

As a result, I got a chance to do some snorkeling, which I'd never done before and always wanted to try. My mom, my sister, and I bought tickets on a tour boat, which took us out to a crescent-shaped island off Maui's coast called Molokini. In truth, it was a partially submerged volcanic crater. Above-ground, it had been proclaimed a bird sanctuary, while below the surface, it was a marine preserve. Humans couldn't set foot on the island, and they weren't supposed to touch the rocks or coral under the water. Tour boats moored in the crescent, and the tourists jumped over the sides of the boats to check out the amazing multicolored fish that called Molokini home.

I was so pumped to get started that I was the first person into the water. I pulled my mask down, put my snorkel in my mouth, put my face in the water, looked down—and immediately felt sick.

No, I hadn't accidentally sucked in some sea water!

I was in thirty feet of water, and it was so clear, I could see straight down to the ocean floor—and I got vertigo. I'm not normally afraid of heights, but I'd never seen a perspective like this, and it freaked me out! I started hyperventilating!

I quickly pulled my face out of the water, took the snorkel from my mouth, and gulped in great breaths of air. One of the tour guides on the boat spotted me and waved me over. I swam back to the side of the boat, and he suggested I grab hold of one of the guide wires mooring us in the island's crescent, then put my face in the water and allow myself to adjust to the view, knowing I had something to hold on to.

I felt a little silly at this point, especially since my mother and my sister were now in the water and swimming around like they were in the shallow end of a community pool, but I did what the guide said. I put my face in the water again and, knowing what to expect this time, felt a little better about it. Slowly, I became used to what I was seeing, my breath resumed a normal pattern, and I swam off behind the rest of my family and enjoyed the remainder of my time at Molokini.

So, being upside down as I faced Apogee, the perspective was strange, but not as strange as it might have been, had I not had my little snorkeling adventure. I didn't have the comfort of a guide wire, but I could tell myself that I wasn't falling, no matter how much I may have felt like it, and I could remind myself to breathe slowly and regularly.

I checked the small readout in the jetpack's handle that indicated how much compressed air I had left for the thrusters. Correcting my spin had taken up more of it than I would have liked. I was going to end this stunt either completely out of oxygen or darn close to it, but it wasn't like I had any other options. "Sandy," I called into the mouthpiece of the Swift Speak, "are you still with me?"

"You bet," she answered right away. "Everything okay?"

"So far, so good." It wasn't exactly the truth, but there was no point getting Sandy more worried than she already was. "Start your distraction anytime."

"You got it," she said, and the next thing I heard was the sound of sirens and a blaring alarm. "One distraction, off and running," she shouted over the noise.

"That sounds like a distraction, all right! What did you do?"

"I set a little fire in the waste-disposal bag and held it up to the smoke alarm! I put the fire out right away, but the smoke alarm doesn't know that! I got the idea from the blaze we had in the shuttle earlier—if that blew *our* minds, I can only imagine what it's doing to Haas in the Command Center!"

"Great thinking! Now try to stay out of trouble. And stay alert. I'm going to need your help and your total knowledge of the specs of Apogee!"

I could almost hear her eyebrow lift up. "Okay," she said. "Whatever you say."

I broke off the communication and returned to the task at hand. Gauging carefully the distance between myself and the space hotel, I held down the thruster button for just as long as I felt I needed. I started to move. I reached peak speed pretty quickly and maintained it, as there was nothing to slow me down. Apogee grew larger and larger before me. I checked the gauge on the jetpack's handle. The compressed-air level was almost down to nothing.

Two things quickly became clear to me: I was moving way too fast, and I wasn't headed directly for the hotel. I was going to come close, but I was going to pass to the left of the central core, with the remaining inflatable modules above me. My heart speeded up, and I could hear my breathing become faster. *Slow down,* I told myself. *Don't hyperventilate. If you pass out, it's all over.*

Getting a Grip

I was going to have one shot at this, and I was going to need all my wits about me. Apogee was close, really close, now. I looked for anything that looked like a handhold on its smooth metal surface. There were ridges in the core, but I wouldn't be able to get enough of a grip on any of them. Then I saw it: a handle. It was attached to a door marked SERVICE ACCESS. Just what I needed!

The handle came at me fast, zooming by on my right as I flew by the door. I stretched out my right hand as far as it could go, leaning my body all the way over, the thrust of my air burst still pushing me forward. I grabbed for the handle and missed. I reached too far, actually, and my wrist hit the thick metal curve. I thought it was all over, but the impact changed my course, and my whole body swerved to the right in a narrow arc, slamming me into the side of the central core.

"Oof!" I grunted, the air knocked out of me. Spots danced in front of my eyes, but I forced myself to see only the handle. I grabbed it and held on tight before my body could rebound off the hull. I lay there and waited for my breath to come back. Raising my head, I could see the inflatable module that had been my room growing smaller and smaller as it drifted farther and farther away from the hotel. Checking my compressed-air gauge again, I saw that it was all the way down to nothing. *So you'd better not fall off the core*, I reminded myself. As if I needed reminding. I tried not to think how close I'd come to shooting right past the station and out on a long trip through the solar system.

"Tom? Did you say something?" I heard Sandy ask. When I didn't reply right away, the tension in her voice increased. "Tom? Tom, talk to me!"

Finally, I had enough breath in my lungs to answer. "I'm here, Sandy. Everything's fine. Okay, now do you remember the specs of the station?"

She actually sounded offended. "Are you kidding?"

"Yes, I'm kidding," I said, adjusting my grip so I could grab on with two hands. I wasn't taking any chances. "I'm at the bottom of the central core on the side with the main antenna. Are there any external cameras on this side?"

Sandy didn't even hesitate. It must be nice to have a photographic memory! "There's one, but it stays fixed on the main antenna. It doesn't move."

"Great," I replied. "I'm coming in a service access door and I'll be working my way up to the Command Center. I'll need you to tell me where the cameras are inside the hotel's core. . . . I don't want Haas to know I'm coming!"

"You got it," she said confidently.

I turned my attention to the access door. The actual lever for it was recessed into the thick metal. It looked heavy; I'd probably need two hands to try to pull it. That was a problem. With both hands in use pulling the handle, I wouldn't be able to anchor myself to the hotel's hull and get extra leverage. But then I had a bright idea. Reaching over, I caught the lever with one hand. Bending a little acrobatically, I was able to hook one foot under the handle I'd been holding, then the other. From here, I was able to get the leverage I'd need to work the lever without worrying about sailing off into space.

I got a good grip with both hands, made sure I was braced, and pulled as hard as I could. The lever moved so easily, I was actually surprised and lost my foothold on the handle! Fortunately, I was hanging on to the lever, which swung outward with the door, and there I was, hanging from it like it was a window ledge.

After slowing my heart down yet again, I slowly worked my way around the side of the door to the inside, and stepped into the service area air lock, pulling the door shut behind me. I sealed it tightly, then pressed the Pressurize button next to it. It glowed red, and a quiet hiss filled the room. Now I had to wait a few minutes while air filled the air lock and the pressure adjusted so it would be safe to remove my suit and helmet. Getting this process down to a few minutes was a pretty recent advance pioneered by Swift Enterprises. Pressurization and adjustment in most space and sea environments usually took several hours.

When the button turned green, the hissing noise ended and I popped the seals on my helmet. It felt great to be out of that thing and, if not breathing fresh air, then at least fresher air than the stuff I'd been breathing since leaving my hotel room. I quickly disconnected my jetpack and took off the rest of my suit, and that's when I realized . . . I hadn't brought my slippers. I was going to have to carry out the rest of my mission floating nearly weightlessly in microgravity. It wouldn't be easy, I knew, especially since I was hardly experienced at moving around under those conditions, but maybe I could turn it to my advantage somehow.

I checked my watch. A half an hour had gone by. Haas's deadline was approaching pretty quickly.

"Sandy, I'm in," I said into my Swift Speak mouthpiece. "But I'm not hearing any fire alarms."

"I think Haas disconnected them," she answered. "He must have figured out there wasn't really a fire."

"Then I'm going to need you to come up with another distraction."

"How?!" she exclaimed, frustrated. "I'm stuck in my room, remember?"

"I don't care, Sandy, you've got to do something," I begged. "All our lives depend on it! I can't have Haas spot me on one of those monitors in the Command Center!"

"All right, all right," she growled. "By the way,

there's a camera in the hall right outside your location. In fact, it's just above your door."

"So if I hug the wall next to the door, the camera won't see me?" I asked.

"I don't think so."

"Excellent. Then I'll get moving. And you're going to find me another distraction, right?"

"Yes," she mumbled. "I think I know a way to do it . . . but I won't like it. . . ."

I left the Swift Speak speaker on to listen to her execute her plan. Personally, I'd be stumped what to do in her situation—coming up with the fire alarm plan had seemed pretty inventive. What could Sandy do to top that, especially given the restrictions of her location?

From the other end of the line, I heard a button being pushed. It sounded like the intercom button. "M-Mister H-H-Haas . . . ?" I heard Sandy whimper tentatively. She sounded like she was on the verge of tears, and I smiled. It must have bugged her so much to play the helpless little kid! My sister was at least as good an actor as I was!

"What is it?" Haas's voice answered back.

"I-I'm scared . . . !"

"That's not my problem. Now clear this line!"

"B-but my b-brother . . . y-you sent him into s-s-space . . . and I don't w-want to b-be next . . . !"

"You won't be next," Haas hissed, clearly annoyed, "as long I get what I want from the people on Earth!"

"I DON'T WANNA DIE," Sandy howled, and I almost couldn't keep myself from laughing. What a performance!

"Okay, okay, settle down," Haas said in a slightly more soothing, less angry voice. He didn't want a freaked-out kid on his hands, after all. But Sandy kept wailing, and I knew he was going to have his hands full with her as long as she kept up her fake hysteria.

I moved to the door, opened it, and slipped into the hall as quietly as I could, even though there wasn't likely to be anyone around, since the entire staff had been confined to their quarters, with the exception of David, who was held hostage with Ms. Fogarty by Haas in the Command Center. But I was in cautious mode, so "tiptoeing" came naturally.

Peeking up, I saw the camera Sandy had mentioned. It was right where she'd said it would be, its unblinking eye keeping watch over the hall. Using the handholds along the wall, I kept myself as flat against it as possible and inched my way to the far side of the corridor, where I opened the door and moved into the next hall. Catching sight of a directory plate, I spoke again into the Swift Speak, whispering this time in case there was any chance Haas might hear me over the intercom speaker. "Sandy, I'm in Corridor C-3. What cameras do I need to look out for?"

I heard her breath hitching, as though she was taking a pause in her out-of-control crying. Under her breath, she whispered, "Two in the corridor, both with blind spots, and they overlap. And then in the next corridor. . . ."

And so it went, with me inching my way along the walls and, when necessary, the floor and the ceiling, following Sandy's directions in corridor after corridor, moving slowly up the levels of Apogee toward the Command Center. The entire way I listened to Sandy hold Haas's attention with wild, faked swings of emotion. The Road Back had never prepared him for anything like Sandy! The poor guy sounded like he was getting close to the end of his rope!

Finally, I came to the corridor that housed the

Command Center. Stealthily, I approached the door. There was no way to get to it without crossing the line of sight of one of the security cameras, so I just had to hope that Sandy's performance was still playing to a mesmerized crowd of one. Figuring out how to get through the door's locking mechanism was going to take some thinking . . . and some time.

But I didn't have time, because a quick check of my watch showed that I only had a few minutes left before Haas made good on his threat to shoot one of his hostages into space.

Haas was thinking the very same thing. Over the Swift Speak, this is what I heard him say: "Enough of this! Go on and cry all you want, I'm sick of trying to shut you up! The hour I gave the idiots on Earth is up in seven minutes—that nosy reporter is going next, if I don't get what I asked for!"

Uh-oh. With Sandy no longer distracting Haas, he was more likely to pay attention to his controls, including the cameras and the monitors that showed what they saw. He was going to see me any second! "Tom," Sandy whispered sharply, "I couldn't hold him any longer! Be careful!"

If only it were going to be that easy!

16

Command Center

Frantically, I looked around the corridor for a place to hide. There were no blind spots for the cameras! The only thing that looked like even a remote possibility was a ventilation duct. It would be a tight fit if I could squeeze myself inside, but I didn't have any other options. I let myself float up to it and examined it. It was secured with simple screws—all I needed was a screwdriver to loosen them.

But I didn't have a screwdriver. Fruitlessly, I pulled at the screws with my fingers, but only succeeded in rubbing my fingers raw. I needed something thin to slide into the screws' slots to turn them—that was the only way this was going to work. But what? The corridor was empty.

And then I remembered something.

I checked all the pockets on my Apogee uniform and found it in my front pants pocket. It was the size of a silver dollar and as thin as . . . the head of a screwdriver.

Joao's medallion.

I looked at the Portuguese poem etched into its surface. "It would be bad if you needed it and didn't have it," he had said. He had no idea how right he was!

Quickly, I set to work and in no time I had the screws removed from the grate. I pulled it off and climbed inside, pulling the grate closed behind me and securing it as best I could, given that I couldn't reattach the screws.

"Three minutes," I heard Haas announce. But I wasn't hearing it through my Swift Speak. Could it be coming from inside the ventilation duct? Twisting my neck, I could see down the duct. Light shone through grate openings at various points along its length.

Somehow, I managed to get myself turned around. I don't know exactly how I did it, but I think I'm probably going to be sore for the rest of my life! I crawled through the duct, doing my best to keep absolutely silent. Coming to one of the grate openings, I peeked through. It was an empty compartment. So was the next one. But the third compartment I found was pay-dirt: the Command Center!

Below me, I could see Haas standing at the command console that housed all of the master controls, with David and Ms. Fogarty sitting tied up nearby. David was struggling with his ropes, but making no progress. Ms. Fogarty was still unconscious. "Two minutes," Haas announced to Earth. "I've got my finger on the button, and when I push it, there'll be one less travel reporter!"

"We're working on it," I heard Giles Burton shout frantically. "We need an extension—even just a couple of minutes!"

Haas shook his head firmly. "Absolutely not," he said. "Let my brothers and sisters in the struggle against technology go, or Elaine Kaufman pays for your inaction!"

I had a moment of panic, wondering how I was going to get the grate open from the inside. After all, the screws were on the *outside*. But I caught a break: Unlike the grate I'd crawled through, this one was secured with simple plastic clasps. I guess the designers figured that if there was an emergency in the Command Center, they didn't want the staff to have to mess around with screws. Whatever the case, I released the clasps silently and pulled the grate inside the duct, laying it quietly to my side.

Now, how was I going to get across the Command Center and surprise Haas without him seeing me? His attention was focused on the console in front of him, so that gave me a little bit of an edge. Then I remembered my *other* edge: I was weightless . . . and suddenly, I thought of a way I *could* put that to good use!

Carefully, I moved out into the Command Center, pulling myself slowly and quietly across the ceiling, upside down, like a spider. Sandy's advice to move according to my center of gravity, along with my experience "walking" in space, had taught me a lot about how to travel in microgravity. I was actually getting pretty good at it! But now was no time to pat myself on the back. "One minute," Haas said into his line to Earth. "I'm waiting to hear good news from you. . . ."

The voice on the other end sounded exhausted. Giles was at his wits' end. This was his worst nightmare, suddenly become reality. "It'll take us at *least* another hour to locate all the Road Back prisoners! You've got to give us more time!"

"No, I don't think so," Haas replied. "If you wanted to save the lives aboard this hotel, you'd find a way to get it done. But I guess you don't, so away poor Ms. Kaufman goes!"

I kept moving, "step" after difficult "step." I was getting closer to where I wanted to be: directly over Haas's head.

"Thirty seconds."

"Wait! Please, wait! Be reasonable!"

Haas snorted. "The way you've been reasonable in dragging all of us into your 'high-tech' society? By forcing us to accept your 'advances' even though everything humanity needs for a perfectly acceptable existence was already here? *I'm* not the unreasonable one! Ten seconds . . . nine . . . eight . . ."

I forced myself to move faster, even though it meant risking making a sound. If Haas saw me, I'd just have to deal with it as best as I could.

". . . seven . . . six . . . five . . ."

His finger moved toward the button that would detach Ms. Kaufman's inflatable room module into space. She didn't have a jetpack that would help save her. I was her only hope.

"... four ... three ... two ..."

I was in position, directly above Haas. I didn't even have time to hope my idea would work.

As hard as I could, I pushed off the ceiling, using my arms and legs to propel me. It was like pushing off the side of a pool, only without the resistance of the water. I was moving really fast and, as there wasn't a whole lot of distance between Haas and me to begin with, I slammed into him like a magazine swatting an unsuspecting fly.

"Oof!" he cried loudly, his arm jostled away from the button at the last second as his body went down in a heap under mine.

"Tom!" David shouted in surprise.

Haas was still wearing his slippers so he could remain "grounded." I held on to him as tightly as I could—he wasn't very big, but he wriggled like a fish in the bottom of a boat!

"Apogee! Apogee, come in!" Giles Burton called from Earth. "What is your status?!"

"Wrestling, Giles!" I yelled, trying to grab hold of Haas's flailing hands.

"Uh . . . say again?" Giles replied, puzzled. "Tom? Is that you? Haas said he ejected you into space!"

"Let me up! Let me up!" insisted Haas, fighting with every ounce of strength he had. Good thing he wasn't very strong. "I must complete my mission!"

"Sorry, that's not going to happen." Finally, I managed to grab both his pinkies in one of my fists. There was no way he was going to get out without breaking his own fingers—a little trick I learned from a bounty hunter while doing research with my dad on a trip through Asia . . . but that's another story.

Haas still struggled as best he could, but I was able to maintain my grip while with my other hand I untied the nylon cord binding David Wong's arms. "Hurry, hurry," he urged. With the knot undone, David shook his arms free, then quickly untied his legs. He came to my assistance and used the cord to tie Haas's hands behind his back.

Haas lay on the floor, cursing us and all of technology. David untied Ms. Fogarty and gently shook her. As she started to come to, David anchored her to her chair with a less confining seat belt. I remained seated on the floor, leaning back against the wall, catching my breath and letting the adrenaline settle in my body.

He looked over at me. "Do I even want to know how you got back here from your ejected module?"

"Probably not," I admitted. "Let's just say I've had a *really* exciting trip, but this hasn't been the most relaxing of vacations!"

We laughed. Hearing us, Haas struggled to roll over and glare at us. "This is *not* over! The Road Back will *never* surrender! We're more determined than you! We're more committed than you! We're smarter than—URK!" He got so excited with his speech that he thrust himself up on his knees, trying to stand forcefully, only to crack his head on the edge of the command console—and knock himself out. He collapsed, and David and I stared at his limp form.

"So much for 'smarter than us,'" I commented.

"I don't mean to interrupt the party," said Giles Burton through the monitor on the Command Console, "but would someone mind telling us what's going on up there?"

"Indeed," said Victoria Fogarty, looking around with half-awake confusion. "What on Earth—or off it—am I doing here and not in my room?"

17

Down to Earth

"That should hold him until the next shuttle gets up here and we can send you all back to Earth," David Wong said. He'd entered a secure lock code into the door panel of an unoccupied guest room module, locking Lars Haas inside. He'd gone in there continuing to rant against technology and the "oppressors of the natural way" as though he'd never knocked himself unconscious. The huge bruise on the top of his forehead said otherwise.

Apogee's crew and the guests had been released from their various rooms, and Sandy, Brendan, Ms. Fogarty, Ms. Kaufman, and a few staff people stood in the hall outside Haas's new quarters. Brendan looked at the closed door. "I want to go in there and punch him out," he said. He turned to look at his mother. "I don't know what I would have done if . . ."

He couldn't finish the sentence, but we understood what he had been about to say. So did Victoria Fogarty. She pulled her son close to her, and he put his arm around her in return. I got the impression that, while it wasn't a pose they'd struck often in the past, they might be doing it a whole lot more in the years to come.

"Instead of freeing his fellow terrorists, Haas is going to get to spend a lot of time with them in prison," Ms. Kaufman said with a smile. "He'll get a long sentence, and I'll get a great story!"

David said, "We just heard from Giles. Above and Beyond says the storm down there is breaking, and the new shuttle will be up here in a few hours. You all may want to go back to your rooms and pack."

"It doesn't seem like we spent any time here at all," Sandy said.

"I know," David said apologetically, "but we've got a lot of work to do up here before we can formally open. We have to add back the two inflatable modules Haas detached, and we have to rethink the communications system on our housekeeping robots. We can't have someone taking them over that easily ever again."

"Did anyone ever find the robot that shocked me?" Ms. Fogarty wanted to know.

"We sure did," David confirmed. "We deactivated all the housekeepers and inspected the recent electrical output of each one individually. It didn't take us long to track down the culprit."

I turned to the travel reporter. "Well, Ms. Kaufman? I guess you're going to slam the space hotel in your review, huh?"

"Well, I don't think it'd be fair to review it just yet," she told me.

"You don't?" Sandy asked, perplexed. "I thought you'd be excited that so many things went wrong!"

Elaine Kaufman smiled. "I know what it may look like, Sandy, but I don't really look for things that are wrong. I mostly look for good stories. And I've got one. But it's not a travel story. I was part of the things that went wrong up here, doing what I did for FUG. I'm really embarrassed about that. It wouldn't be fair of me to write a review under these circumstances."

I admit Ms. Kaufman surprised me. I knew some of it was that she didn't want to get in trouble for spying for Foger Utility Group, but there was a part of her that sounded sincere, too.

"Like Mr. Wong said, there's still a lot to be done up here before the place can open," she continued. "And I think it might be best to give the hotel another test run for a preliminary review once all that's finished. A review written by another reporter."

David smiled gratefully. "I think that's absolutely the right way to go."

That night, our return shuttle glided gracefully back to a private Above and Beyond landing strip near Rio. Sandy and I were both exhausted, and we still had more traveling to go. Our father had been understandably rattled when he heard what had happened on Apogee, and he had sent a Swift jet to pick us up at the Rio airport and fly us back home as soon as possible.

Having turned in our space suits, we moved slowly through the Above and Beyond headquarters. Our weariness plus the return of gravity's effects on our bodies made us feel like we were walking through quicksand.

Brendan's father had met us at the headquarters, and enveloped his wife and son in a tight hug. Any tension or distance they'd had as a family before certainly wasn't there now.

Ms. Kaufman went straight for the nearest telephone and started dictating her story into the receiver. It sounded like it was going to be a dramatic tale: "The saboteur's heart was as black as space," I heard her say. I rolled my eyes.

FBI agents were waiting with Giles Burton for us as soon as the shuttle's hatch opened and we stepped out into the warm moonlight. Giles scooped us up in excruciatingly painful hugs that we didn't mind at all. He was glad to see us, and we were more than glad to see him.

As the FBI agents took custody of Haas, putting him in proper handcuffs, they told us they'd located the real Dr. Gorinsky and rescued him from the Road Back cell that had kidnapped him. And he had a beard after all, and absolutely remembered meeting Ms. Fogarty years before. Heck, with all the money she'd been throwing around, she *was* pretty unforgettable. As the agents steered him to a waiting black car, Haas berated them with antitechnology rants the entire way. I was glad he was someone else's problem now!

Sandy and I had nearly made it to the front door of Above and Beyond, our eyelids drooping like they weighed a thousand pounds each, when a staffer trotted up and stepped in front of us. "Glad I caught you before you left," she said. "You've got a video call."

"It's probably Dad," I said to Sandy through a yawn.

We followed the staffer to a video terminal. She punched a few buttons, and David Wong's face appeared on the monitor. He smiled. "I just wanted to make sure you made it back all right," he said.

"We're here," I replied.

"We're half awake, but we're here," Sandy chipped in.

"I also wanted to thank you both," David said seriously. "If it weren't for the two of you, I don't know what would have happened. You saved the entire Apogee project."

"Apogee is too cool to let someone mess it up," I told him.

"It's just . . . I've put so many years into this space hotel . . . I wish there was some way I could repay you. . . ."

"You could let us come back and stay for free," Sandy suggested. All three of us laughed. Given Swift Enterprises' involvement in the project, it was doubtful we'd ever have to pay if we returned to Apogee, even if we wanted to.

"We really do want to come back," I said. "In fact, I can't wait! Among other things, I owe Sandy a rematch at badminton!"

David smiled again. "You're always welcome up here," he assured us. "Have a safe trip home." He clicked off, and the screen went dark.

We turned and headed for the door again. Sandy yawned. "'Safe trip'? After what we've been through, I can't imagine any way the rest of our trip could be dangerous!"

The doors whooshed open, and the humid air of the Brazilian night enveloped us. And there, standing before us, was the one thing that could add the element of danger Sandy couldn't imagine.

"Hey! You are back!" Joao exclaimed, clapping his hands, then holding them up for us. "Give me high five!"

Wearily, we smiled and did as he asked, and he wrapped us up in a big, joyous hug. "I was so worried about you when I heard what was happening up there. Are you okay?"

"We're fine, Joao," Sandy said. "It's good to see you."

"And it's good to see you!" He elbowed me so hard, I almost fell over—that's how tired I was. "I guess my medallion really did protect you, huh?"

I fished it out of my pocket and handed it to him. "It did a lot more than that, Joao. If I hadn't had it, we might not be having this conversation right now. Thank you," I said sincerely.

Joao looked at me, puzzled. "It is a good medallion, but I didn't know it was *that* good. . . ."

He reached for our bags and took them to the trunk of his waiting car. Sandy and I climbed into the backseat, slumping down against it, our eyes already beginning to close. Joao took his place behind the steering wheel and started the engine. "Ooh," he said, examining us in the rearview mirror. "You look very tired. I will be sure to give you a nice, smooth ride to the airport."

"That," my sister and I said together, "would be great."

Joao started the car, then gunned the engine fearsomely and the car screeched as it moved away from the curb. Our eyes flew open like pulled window shade. *Nothing about this trip has been "nice and smooth,"* I thought, unable to keep myself from smiling. *No reason to start now!*